THE CONSPIRACIES OF THE EMPIRE

Also by Qiu Xiaolong

A Judge Dee Investigation

THE SHADOW OF THE EMPIRE *

The Inspector Chen mysteries

DEATH OF A RED HEROINE
A LOYAL CHARACTER DANCER
WHEN RED IS BLACK
A CASE OF TWO CITIES
RED MANDARIN DRESS
THE MAO CASE
YEARS OF RED DUST (*short story collection*)
DON'T CRY, TAI LAKE
THE ENIGMA OF CHINA
SHANGHAI REDEMPTION
HOLD YOUR BREATH, CHINA *
BECOMING INSPECTOR CHEN *
INSPECTOR CHEN AND THE PRIVATE KITCHEN MURDER *
LOVE AND MURDER IN THE TIME OF COVID *

* *available from Severn House*

THE CONSPIRACIES OF THE EMPIRE

Qiu Xiaolong

SEVERN
HOUSE

First world edition published in Great Britain and the USA in 2024
by Severn House, an imprint of Canongate Books Ltd,
14 High Street, Edinburgh EH1 1TE.

severnhouse.com

British Library Cataloguing-in-Publication Data
A CIP catalogue record for this title is available from the British Library.

ISBN-13: 978-1-4483-1308-2 (cased)
ISBN-13: 978-1-4483-1482-9 (e-book)

All Severn House titles are printed on acid-free paper.

Typeset by Palimpsest Book Production Ltd., Falkirk,
Stirlingshire, Scotland.
Printed and bound in Great Britain by TJ Books,
Padstow, Cornwall.

Praise for the Judge Dee Investigation novels

"Qiu combines a sophisticated puzzle with appropriate period detail, avoiding the anachronisms of previous Judge Dee fiction. Fans of those books, by Robert van Gulik and others, will clamor for more"
Publishers Weekly Starred Review

"Qiu writes in a lyrical style . . . Poems become clues, even evidence, in the far-from-cursory probe he conducts"
Wall Street Journal

"An elaborate and satisfying souffle of mystery, history, and poetry"
Kirkus Reviews

"Qiu's rendition [of Judge Dee] is just as approachable and good-natured as his contemporary murder mysteries"
The Asian Review of Books

"Judge Dee and Yang are an endearing duo for this delightful series"
The Historical Novels Review

About the author

Anthony Award-winning author **Qiu Xiaolong** was born in Shanghai and moved to Washington University in St Louis, US, to complete a PhD degree in comparative literature. After the Tiananmen tragedy in 1989 he stayed on in St Louis where he still lives with his wife.

As well as his new mystery series set in Tang dynasty China, featuring the legendary Judge Dee Renjie, Qiu is the author of the renowned Inspector Chen mysteries, which have sold over two million copies worldwide and been published in twenty languages. The Chen novels have all been adapted as BBC Radio 4 dramas. On top of his fiction, he is a prize-winning writer of poetry and a poetry critic.

www.qiuxiaolong.com

ONE

'The things you really need are few and easy to come by; but the things you can imagine you need are infinite, and you will never be satisfied.'

– Epicurus

'The individual has always had to struggle to keep from being overwhelmed by the tribe. If you try it, you will be lonely often, and sometimes frightened. But no price is too high to pay for the privilege of owning yourself.'

– Rudyard Kipling

'The curfew tolls the knell of parting day;
The lowing herd wind slowly o'er the lea,
The plowman homeward plods his weary way,
And leaves the world to darkness and to me.'

– Thomas Gray

Dee Renjie, commonly known as Judge Dee in the Great Tang Empire, woke with a start from a horrible nightmare.

Rubbing his eyes in disorientation, he found his silk sleeping robe was drenched in cold, clammy sweat. The ominous dream scenes were already fading, like ignorant armies clashing in the confusion of the fast-retreating dark of night.

The candle on the mahogany bedside table had burned itself out, leaving droplets of white wax scattered around, and a faint smell was still hanging in the air. The early-morning light was stumbling in through the bamboo paper window.

A fragment of the dream seemed to be still lingering in his memory, and Judge Dee tried hard to recall it, stroking his white-streaked beard.

In his mind's eye, he could see a creature with the scarlet head of a fox connected to the white body of a snake. It was moaning, its voluptuous round belly twitching, writhing, as it circled a golden dragon-engraved pillar in the palace, twirling non-stop like a wanton pole dancer. Behind the soaring golden dragon, in the heart of the magnificent court of the great Tang Empire, was a splendid golden throne . . .

Judge Dee heard a cock crowing in the distance, quickly followed by a knock on his bedroom door.

'Just a minute. I'm putting on some clothes.' Judge Dee hurriedly took off his sweat-drenched sleeping robe and changed into a new gray cotton gown.

When he had changed, his servant Yang pushed open the door and entered the room, worry written all over his face.

'I heard you screaming, Master.'

'It was nothing but a bad dream.'

'A bad dream on the day you have to leave the capital to carry out a new investigation? That may not be such an auspicious sign, Master. The investigation is about a missing person, a poet named Luo Binwang, am I right?'

Having grown up in a remote, backward Shandong village, Yang remained full of superstitious, supernatural beliefs, despite the years he'd spent in Dee's company.

'Don't worry, Yang. "Confucius says, you don't need to talk about anything superstitious or supernatural."'

'It's not your job to search all over the country for a nobody like Luo,' Yang continued, shaking his head and frowning in spite of himself. 'I don't know what Her Majesty's problem is.'

'No, Luo Binwang is far from being a nobody. He wrote the unbelievably influential "Call to Arms" during the recent uprising under General Xu against Her Majesty. This well-written poem swelled the rebellion's armies. Indeed! Such a brilliant masterpiece! It's said that Her Majesty broke out in a cold sweat halfway through reading it. She scolded me for not having recommended Luo, a poet endowed with such talent, to her earlier. And she provided me with some information about the investigation into the mysterious disappearance of Luo Binwang.'

'That's hard to believe. Her dramatic reaction, I mean.'

'She's eager to have talented people serving under her administration. That's not unbelievable.' In fact, Judge Dee himself did not really believe that. It was more than possible that the empress wanted revenge against Luo for the role he had played in the rebellion. So instead of continuing the conversation further in that direction, Judge Dee changed the topic, merely saying, 'Between you and me, the mission in front of us is by no means simple.'

'Why not, Master?'

'It may be just a hunch on my part; I cannot tell exactly at the present moment. Not at this stage of the investigation.'

After Yang left the room, Judge Dee caught himself staring at the bare, crumbling wall again. It revealed no traces of the dream scene – of the horrible monster with its scarlet fox head and white snake body, winding itself around a golden palace pillar. Judge Dee did not believe in the interpretation of dreams. The practice was too weird to have any truth. Nonetheless, the symbolism of that dream scene filled his heart with trepidation.

It could have a lot to do, he contemplated, with the special case Empress Wu had just assigned him the previous day. After the rebellion was quashed, the poet Luo Binwang had vanished, but his body had not been recovered from the battlefield. Was he dead or alive? No one seemed to know for sure.

'You go and find out what happened to Luo Binwang for me. What a great talent Luo really is!' the empress had said to him sternly, sitting on the resplendent throne. As an extraordinary favor, in consideration of his age, Judge Dee was allowed to seat himself on a stool beneath her, instead of standing straight like other officials in the court. 'If Luo's still alive, bring him back, and if he's dead, bring back his body. After all, you have to do this job for me because you failed in your duty to recommend Luo to me before he wrote his "Call to Arms", Judge Dee.'

'Yes, it is my responsibility, Your Majesty,' he said, standing up in a fluster. It was no secret that Empress Wu did not like Luo at all, having once thrown him in prison, long before he wrote his 'Call to Arms'. Judge Dee saw no point, however, in arguing with the empress. 'I'm old, decrepit and worn out, with so many things on my hands. You know only too well how it is, Your Majesty. I should have stepped down from my position long ago.'

'Don't say that to me, my capable Judge Dee. I'm not holding you responsible for Luo's "Call to Arms". Let me tell you my experience of reading it for the first time. I was sick with a headache, but halfway through that poem, I broke out in a cold sweat. Believe it or not, it cured my headache miraculously in no time. So you have to ferret him out for me! You're the only one I can trust for the job. You know you cannot say no to me, Judge Dee.'

She produced a mini scroll and held it out to Judge Dee, without letting him reply. 'What a masterpiece is this poem "Ode to a Cicada in Prison"! Luo Binwang wrote it, long before he joined the rebellion. You must have read it before.'

The judge took the scroll from her, spread it out and began to read in earnest, frowning:

In the fall, you begin to sing
to a captive overwhelmed by worries.
It is unbearable to hear you scratching
your black wings in a sad song
to a white-haired prisoner like me.
The autumn dew drops falling,
falling too heavy, you cannot fly high.
The cold wind drowns your melody.
Who comes to believe you're so noble
and pure? Who comes to address
all the grievous wrongs afflicted
on an innocent man like me?

'I am ashamed to say I have not read it before, Your Majesty. If I had, I might have been able to talk with Luo, about whatever wrongs he was complaining of in the poem.'

'It was apparent,' she said, shaking her head under the heavy gold crown of the empress, 'that he harbored resentment against me. It's really my oversight.'

'No, it's mine, Your Majesty. I'm getting too old, and I've

been overburdened with work all these years. It would be too difficult for me to carry out the investigation. It's time for a younger person to take the job.' Judge Dee went on after a short pause, 'Besides, I don't have a detailed file on his disappearance. For instance, where are the likely places he could be hiding? Or who are the people he might contact while running away from the last battlefield?'

'The last battle has been so recently fought, Judge Dee. The information is still coming, dripping in. I don't have anything that detailed, but I'll manage to keep you posted with anything new.'

Luo Binwang's disappearance was a complicated case with an even more complicated political background, Judge Dee knew. Could that be the reason why the empress chose not to give him any detailed or reliable information? As the old Chinese saying went, the case was full of conspiracies and casualties caused by misplaced Yin and Yang – and solving it involved taking a walk through a dark, deceptive, secret corridor of the Tang Empire's recent history.

After the death of the late Emperor Gaozhong, Empress Wu had become the supreme ruler. That was unacceptable to some of the orthodox Confucianist scholars-turned-officials, even though, under her rule, the Tang Empire was enjoying a period of unprecedented prosperity. To make things even worse, Wu ruled in a cruel and controversial way. It was rumored that she had deviously framed the previous Empress Wang for the murder of Wu's own infant daughter, thereby clearing her path to ascend to the supreme empress position, and that she'd also exiled the crown prince using false pretexts, in a devious attempt to further consolidate her own power base . . .

All that had led to the recent uprising against the empress led by General Xu Jingye, at the beginning of which Luo Binwang had composed his high-spirited 'Call to Arms'. It had turned out to be an influential and inspiring piece, thanks to which more than ten thousand people were reported to have joined the rebellious army during the first week alone.

As for the empress's criticism regarding Judge Dee's failure to recommend Luo earlier to her, it was unexpected, but the judge was not entirely surprised. The empress was, of course, in a strong position to say such a thing, regardless of her real feelings. Whatever problems she might have, she was known for her genuine eagerness to gather talented officials around her. For the welfare of the Great Tang dynasty, she had paid sincere respect to many honest, capable officials in her court, even though some of them were critical of her policies and iron rule. It was a fairly small circle, that included Judge Dee himself.

And Judge Dee had learned this from his own experience. One day, she was alleged to be sleeping with a gigolo in the royal bedchamber, he remembered, but upon hearing that Dee had an urgent report for her concerning the stability of the Tang Empire, she hurried out barefoot, her face flushed, her hair disheveled, to meet with him there and then for a long, serious discussion.

In reality, Judge Dee was a top-ranking minister at court rather than a judge. But, having successfully solved a number of sensitive political cases that had proved to be too difficult to others, he was now simply called Judge Dee by many people. He had been pushed into the position because there was no independent judicial system in the Tang Empire. One had to be an official with executive power in order to carry out a judicial investigation in an effective way.

Dee Renjie himself had no objection to the neutral title. 'Judge Dee' sounded somehow distanced from politics. In these days of increasingly fierce, cut-throat power struggles at the Tang imperial court between the Wu and Li families, the title of 'judge' was seemingly acceptable to both factions. And it was acceptable to Dee himself too, he reflected, pulling himself out of his memories and back into the present.

The morning light was now streaming in through the white paper window of his bedroom. Judge Dee folded his hands around a cup of Dragon Well tea and took a sip, before adjusting his official cap in an ancient bronze mirror. He was ready to begin preparations for the day's work concerning Luo Binwang.

Luo Binwang was not a political poet, except for the rhapsody-like piece titled 'Call to Arms'. Judge Dee, sitting upright in a bamboo chair in his bedroom, brooded pensively over how to take the first step in the investigation. Could Luo Binwang really have been a talented official? Judge Dee was not so sure about that.

To say the least, Luo had not had a successful official career. His prospects had been marred on account of his having been once thrown into prison for a short period. His arrest was attributed to some less-than-wise remarks regarding the empress. And then, of course, he'd made the even more unwise decision to join the rebellion under General Xu, which had failed miserably. He had both chosen the wrong time and made a wrong calculation of the situation.

At present, however, Luo presented no real threat to Empress Wu. Not anymore. Not after the disastrous defeat suffered by the rebellion's army by the Wuding River. Even the ringleader, General Xu, had been killed in that final battle.

Judge Dee saw no convincing justification for the urgency expressed by the empress – not for an investigation into the disappearance of an aged, feeble poet like Luo Binwang, who, as in the old Chinese saying, did not have the strength to kill a chicken.

But Judge Dee was not in a position to say no to the empress. Nor to ask her why she placed so much importance on finding Luo now. He knew only too well about all the political hazards behind the case, and that investigating it was so difficult, possibly a devious trap for him too.

So, all that Judge Dee could do was hunt out Luo in one way or another – or, failing that, find his unmistakable dead body.

It was a tall order. In the official documents, Luo was listed as missing in the last battle, but his body had never been found – either on the battlefield in question or somewhere else entirely – in spite of the relentless searching all over the country that had already been carried out under the empress's orders.

Most people maintained that Luo Binwang was dead, his body trampled out of recognition on the battlefield close to the Wuding River. More likely than not, Judge Dee contemplated in silence, this further search he'd been ordered to make was just for show, performed out of political considerations, and he was not expected to actually find Luo – alive *or* dead. The empress had repeatedly demonstrated in public that she valued talent more than anything else in the world. Judge Dee did not know if these were her real feelings; it could have been staged for her image as a wise empress, working wholeheartedly for the welfare of the great Tang Empire. Either way, her decision to send Judge Dee himself in search of Luo Binwang had been made, paradoxical though it might seem, despite his vehement denouncement of her in the 'Call to Arms'.

What theories, what clues were there for Judge Dee to follow in his missing-person investigation?

Luo's parents were both dead, and he was their only son. He had a younger sister, who had fallen out with him, but other than that he only had a few distant relatives, who he'd long been out of touch with. No immediate information from them, needless to say. That wasn't too surprising. Whatever their real relationship, the people related to him now had to put on a show of having long avoided him like the black plague after his imprisonment for slandering the empress, not to mention his more recent role in the armed uprising against her.

No, after considering the facts, Judge Dee concluded that the most likely reason for Luo Binwang's disappearance was that he'd been killed in the failed rebellion.

But there was another possible scenario he could not afford to rule out. Luo could have run away in the chaos of the battlefield and was, even now, keeping himself hidden somewhere. An old Chinese saying put it well: a shrewd rabbit keeps three dens to hide itself in, if need be. Although this seemed improbable, Judge Dee thought he had no choice but to explore the case in that direction as well.

All in all, Judge Dee reflected, it appeared to be an extremely difficult job. And to make matters even trickier, although he had long been aware of Luo in his status as a famous poet, Dee had not met him in person, nor made a serious study of any of his poems. There was, therefore, a lot of background information for him to gather and sort through in a great hurry.

Judge Dee had promised the empress that he was going to leave to start his investigation the next day. So far, he had not even decided, however, where he would make his first stop out of the great capital of Chang'an.

'This morning,' Judge Dee said, turning to his loyal assistant Yang, who was standing, still rubbing his hands in anxiety, in Dee's room, 'you don't have to stay with me. I am going to see Academician Jiong, and we'll probably have quite a long talk. But there are a couple of things you can do for me. First, go and find a copy of Luo Binwang's poetry collection. That may turn out to be helpful for the investigation.'

'I'll set out for the job immediately, if you insist, but you must be really careful, Master,' Yang said, showing no rush to leave.

It might not be an easy job for Yang, Judge Dee thought. He was no bookworm like his master, nor did he frequent any bookstores.

'As far as I know, people buy and sell books, both new and second-hand, mostly in temple market fairs,' Yang grumbled. 'I have no idea, however, about when and where those market fairs are held. Only once, I remember, have I followed you into something like a bookstore in the center of the capital. But that bookstore seems to be located a bit too far away, so—'

'Then you'll have to hurry, Yang. Afterward, arrange for me to have a late lunch in a restaurant's private room. In absolute privacy, mind you. And bring my lunch guest, a woman surnamed Ning, directly to the restaurant you have booked. She lives in a hut near the "outer palace". Ning once served as a personal maid to the former Empress Wang. Make sure that no one will notice anything unusual or be suspicious about the arrangement, and under no circumstances should you reveal either your identity or mine.'

'Got you, Master.'

Once Yang's heavy footsteps were fading away, Judge Dee glanced out the window and watched, as if in a trance, a large leaf falling, swirling down to the courtyard.

He knew what was behind Yang's grumpiness about the investigation. In her earlier days, Empress Wu had once served as a 'palace female talent' for Emperor Taizhong of the Tang Empire. It was conventional that after an emperor's death, each and every one of his palace women would have to live in seclusion, spending the rest of their lives together in government-controlled isolation. They were seen as touched by the emperor, hence untouchable by other men. A number of the palace ladies, like Wu, were sent to live in nunneries.

However, the new emperor – Li Zhi, the son of the late emperor – fell head over heels in love with Wu. One thing led to another, and despite being a 'palace female talent' for the late emperor, Wu became an imperial concubine for the young emperor too – a dramatic turn of events so scandalous that it was intolerable to the orthodox Confucianist officials.

She was subsequently declared to be the empress, and after the death of Li Zhi, she eventually seated herself on the throne as supreme ruler of the whole nation. Of late, she had even gone so far as to try to rename the Tang Empire as the Zhou Empire, and to move China's capital from the city of Chang'an to the city of Luoyang.

This metamorphosis was naturally unacceptable to the people who had pledged allegiance to the Li family's Tang Empire. And, as a result, the rebellion under General Xu had broken out, but without success.

It was ironic that Judge Dee himself happened to be both a traditional Confucianist scholar and, at the same time, a senior, highly trusted official serving under Empress Wu. But it was much simpler for Yang. He just resented the fact that his aged master had been ordered around, for one investigation after another.

It did not take Yang long to reach the center of the city. There, to his confusion, he failed to recognize the bookstore he had visited before in the company of Judge Dee. And to his further dismay, he did not find any bookstores selling poetry collections. In fact, most of the bookstores he came across carried only textbooks of Confucian classics, such as *Analects*, *Book of Rites*, *Book of Songs* and *Book of Changes*.

After several unsuccessful attempts, he finally spotted something that seemed like a rare book section in a dust-covered corner of a medium-sized store outside of the city center, sporting several author-handwritten copies on display. The section was overshadowed, though, by an impressive array of silk scrolls of poems and paintings, hanging down vertically from the top of the white wall.

According to the bookstore owner, who introduced himself as Fatty Bao, local poets and writers would occasionally put a few loose pages of their handwritten manuscripts on sale there, commonly made in the form of silk scrolls to be hung in the living room for decoration. Fatty Bao did not carry anything close to a complete or well-edited poetry collection.

'A woodblock-printed edition can be very expensive. An individual poet's collection often has only a very small print run. It is far from enough to cover the cost of woodblock printing. Ordinary poets could not afford that.'

'Do you have any poems left by Luo Binwang?' Yang asked directly. 'Separate pieces, whether in his own calligraphy or not. Like in the form of a silk scroll?'

'Luo Binwang? Oh, no. We might have had one or two silk scrolls of his poems once. But all of a sudden, his poems became very valuable, and despite the high prices, they sold out in no time.'

In light of what Judge Dee had told him regarding the Luo case, Yang thought he had a good idea of the reasons behind the unexpected rise in the value of Luo Binwang's poems. But thinking about this reminded him of another investigation Judge Dee had conducted in his company, concerning a poetess instead of a poet. In that case, her poems had turned out to be vital for the investigation, he recalled. He had to get hold of Luo's poems for his master, by hook or by crook.

Shifting his glance to a long silk scroll hung on the wall with quite a high price tag, Yang wondered whether Luo's scrolls had all really sold out so quickly. Fatty Bao could still secretly own some of them, waiting so that he could sell them for an even higher price in the future.

'You know who sent me here, Fatty Bao?' Yang asked.

'I don't know.'

'None other than Judge Dee.'

'Oh, His Honor still remembers me? Indeed, what a big and fatty face I must have today.'

'The empress has just forced a politically sensitive case on him. He is to find the missing Luo Binwang for her. If I fail to learn anything from you, I may have no choice but to tell the secret police that you once had several scrolls of his poems in your store. And I think that they will move mountains and seas to dig out anything related that's still in your shop. You can count on that, Fatty Bao.'

'Hold on, Yang! You should have told me earlier about Judge Dee's investigation.'

Fatty Bao spun around to climb into the attic and soon came back down helter-skelter, carefully holding a handwritten silk scroll. It was a poem composed on the occasion of Luo's parting with a friend, and appeared to have been handwritten by Luo Binwang himself. Toward the left bottom of the scroll, there was a line written in smaller characters: 'Copied out for Yu.'

Yang took the scroll from Fatty Bao's hand. He was no judge of the monetary value of poetry, but the silk scroll was marked with an incredibly high price, which could have been added recently.

'For Judge Dee, it's absolutely free,' Fatty Bao said with an obsequious smile, tearing off the price tag in haste. 'I have always been an admirer of His Honor. What a high-ranking official at the court, full of political integrity and passion for justice!'

It was a shrewd move on Fatty Bao's part. Judge Dee was not just a judge but also a powerful high-ranking minister, and was highly trusted by the empress. Yang did not think Fatty Bao needed to go into detail about his decision.

After walking out of the bookstore, Yang found the scroll of Luo's poem tucked under his arm unexpectedly helpful to his further inquiries. It provided him with convincing proof that he was genuinely looking to buy Luo's poems – or, failing that, a reasonable pretext for why he was making inquiries about the disgraced poet.

Still, people avoided talking about Luo like the black plague. Those Yang approached were invariably like ravens trembling in the chilly winter, their tongues frozen.

Yang remembered Judge Dee once talking to him about the horror of 'literature prison'. People knew that anything related to Luo could get them into serious political trouble. The secret police would come knocking noisily on their doors, both day and night, like tireless woodpeckers in the dark woods.

While Yang was searching for poems that morning, Judge Dee had himself carried in a vermilion-painted bamboo sedan chair to the residence of the renowned poet Jiong Yang. The first step in the investigation into Luo's disappearance.

Among the 'four most excellent poets' – Wang Bo, Luo Binwang, Jiong Yang, Lu Yinglun – of the early Tang dynasty, Jiong alone shared a number of similarities with Luo.

For one thing, both of the two men's aspirations were apparently not confined to poetry writing. On the contrary, they actually considered poets like themselves to be useless in the turbulent times. That's how Jiong came to write the well-known couplet:

O, I would rather be a petty officer fighting
than a useless scholar writing.

As for Luo Binwang, his choice to join the rebellious army as a soldier spoke volumes. Not to mention the group of poems he had written about army life on the borders as well as on the battlefields.

Jiong hurried out the door of his residence to meet Judge Dee. He greeted him with a long bow and led the 'distinguished visitor' cordially into his spacious study.

There was a large, shining mahogany table in the center of the room, which was lined with custom-made mahogany bookshelves full of books, as well as mahogany display cabinets carved with intricate patterns. Jiong himself prepared Judge Dee a cup of Red Robe Tea on the mahogany tea-stand.

'I have to apologize for my unannounced visit today, Academician Jiong,' Judge Dee said. 'You are one of the most distinguished scholars in the Tang Imperial Academy, and a famous poet as well. I know only too well how busy you must be.'

Jiong had come out with flying colors in the civil service examination at the capital level. He was then enlisted into the

Imperial Academy. Academician was a position with a lot of honor, but not too much real power. From there, however, it was not unimaginable that an academician might soon be assigned to another position with power as well as honor.

'We are both serving under Her Majesty, Your Honor,' Jiong said, 'and I surely know how much busier you must be at your higher position. Coincidentally, I've just heard about the new case Her Majesty has assigned you, so I have been anticipating your visit. It's about Luo Binwang, right?'

'Yes, Jiong, I'm investigating his disappearance, and I'm utterly clueless about the case. So anything you can tell me about Luo will prove to be of great help. You know him, do you not?'

'Well, it's true that Luo and I have talked from time to time, and exchanged our poems with each other. It's possibly because of our similar poetic sensibilities, I suppose. To put it another way, it's also because of our common aspiration to do something more than compose a couple of sentimental, useless lines.'

'Yes, I like that uplifting poem of yours entitled "Army Song". What a masterpiece indeed!' Judge Dee stood up, and recited the poem in the study from memory, beside a clay sculpture of a solitary, upright soldier, shining on the dark wood bookshelf:

The beacon fire already reaching the Western Capital,
our hearts are full of indignation.
Bidding farewell to the palace,
the general leaves with the emperor's order,
and the soldiers fight bravely against the enemy
surrounding and attacking our city.
The heavy snow eclipsing the banners,
the battle drums adding to the howling wind.
O, I would rather be a petty officer fighting
than a useless scholar writing.

'You remember those lines so well, Your Honor,' Jiong said. 'I truly appreciate it.'

'And I truly appreciate this masterpiece of yours. In fact, I often recite the last couplet to myself. It's so inspiring, and thought-provoking too, in these turbulent times.'

'Luo also wrote a number of poems in a similar style. He and I are both listed as "Border Poets" by some critics, for our common focus on the battles and army experiences on the borders. His are slightly different from mine, with a more somber, realistic tone. That seems quite understandable to me, though. Luo has suffered too many frustrations and setbacks in his career. It's said he made some inappropriate remarks in the past, which more than angered the empress, and he was consequently thrown into jail for a short while.'

'Yes, I've heard something about his bad luck, but I'm not too clear about the details. I did not know him personally, you understand.'

'He's an unorthodox poet,' Jiong said delicately. 'That could have accounted – at least partially – for his bad luck. From time to time, we talked and discussed poetry, but that does not mean we're inclined toward the same political stance.'

'I understand, Jiong.'

'In fact, before the start of the uprising, he never revealed anything to me about General Xu or the forthcoming rebellion. Nor did he ever mention anything about his plan to participate in the disastrous attempt, let alone his composition in secret of that well-known poem "Call to Arms". Not a single word about it. After all, I am far from being close to him.'

Jiong had to highlight his distance from Luo. Judge Dee more than understood the necessity of it. The 'literature prison' under Empress Wu had stricken terror deep into the hearts of so many men of letters – including Judge Dee himself.

'What's wrong with poets meeting and discussing their works?' Judge Dee said. 'That's what literature is about. It does not mean they share the same political stance. Not at all, I have to say in all seriousness.'

'Thank you so much for your perceptive understanding, Your Honor,' Jiong said.

'I've recently learned from Her Majesty that Luo had a poem titled "Ode to a Cicada in Prison." Was that poem composed after he had fallen out with the empress?'

'It's a masterpiece, Your Honor. The man and the cicada are perfectly juxtaposed in the lines. I'm not too sure exactly when he wrote it, but judging from the title, yes, he must have written it in prison after he had offended Her Majesty.'

'That explains a lot. Especially his decision to join the rebellion—'

Their talk was interrupted by a young servant, who placed several cold dishes and a dainty kettle of Shaoxing rice wine on a small portable mahogany table between the two of them.

'One more question I have to ask you, Jiong,' Judge Dee resumed after the servant withdrew out of sight. 'Do you know anyone really close to, or intimate with, Luo Binwang? Not necessarily just in the capital, I mean.'

'That I do not know. But,' Jiong added after a short pause, frowning, 'now you mention it, I've heard tales about a fishing girl in the Shu River area who might have been quite close to Luo at one time. As far as I know, Luo spent a couple of days in her boat. It's said that one of his poems – a hot, romantic one – was written for her, despite the age difference between the two of them, and that other poems inspired by her may be in existence.'

'Really? Thank you so much, Academician Jiong! I've never heard or read anything about it.'

'I think I can dig the poem out for you. I mean, if you're interested in it.'

'Of course I'm interested; that would be fantastic. Can you tell me more about the girl and the poem?'

'It was probably written prior to his prison days. Luo was in his early or mid-fifties at the time, but he remained single. Like other romantic poets, he'd had occasional affairs with women, sometimes in places of ill repute . . .'

'Does that include the fishing girl in question?'

'She's not exactly in an illicit business, but there're stories about the obscure way she makes money.'

'That's intriguing. Normally, a fishing girl does the simple job of catching fish and selling them to customers, right?'

'Well, she does much more than that,' Jiong said, tossing a wok-fried peanut into his mouth before taking another long sip of amber-colored rice wine. 'She has a sampan – a flat-bottomed wooden boat – under her name, in which she prepares so-called "boat dinners" for her customers. All the chef specials are made out of fresh, live catches from the river on that day. The gourmet customers cannot help but come crowding over to her, like moths flying to the light.'

'That surely sounds tantalizing, Jiong. But what if she fails to make any catches for the day?'

'She's said to be an extraordinary swimmer, gliding over the water like a flying fish, and diving like a mermaid too. If needs be, she would jump into the river there and then, and is capable of catching a live fish with her bare hands in less than five minutes.

'The meal is, of course, delicious, according to gourmet critics, but rumored to be even more delicious is the young girl herself. When she's jumping out of the river, shaking beads of water from her half-naked body and long wet black hair, stamping her bare feet on the sampan deck, her *dudou*-like corset clinging to her youthful body, bringing out all the curves, how could her customers even hope to resist such a delicious temptation?'

'Well, Confucius says, it's human nature to be after both delicious food and delicious girls,' Judge Dee responded with a chuckle. It was a parody of Confucius, but it was also not that far-fetched. That was one of the problems with Confucianism, Dee thought: its maxims could be so generalized, open to various interpretations. 'Are there any other things out of the ordinary about that special sampan meal of hers?'

'Well, after the dinner – I mean one-to-one dinner, you know – rumor has it that she decides whether or not to let the customer stay overnight with her, alone in the boat. That's one thing those customers of her boat told me. She does not let *all* the customers stay.'

'But she allowed Luo to do so?'

'Apparently, she did. And not only for one night, but for a couple of nights. Not to mention the fact that she must have cooked him three special meals per day for free on the sampan as well. Luo was too poor to be able to afford her prices. The special sampan meals cost a lot.'

'This is getting more and more intriguing. A beauty who truly understands the music indeed. As far as I know, Luo has never been a well-to-do man.'

'You mean the lovers who truly understand each other like the music they are playing? I think I have read that metaphor in a book written in the Spring and Autumn period. Back to the fishing girl, her decisions may not necessarily depend on how much a customer pays her.'

'She certainly sounds like an interesting character,' Judge Dee said. 'Thank you so much, Jiong. I have learned a lot from you today, but I have to leave for another appointment now. Her Majesty wants me to set out tomorrow morning in search of Luo.'

'Yes, you have such a lot on your hands, I understand. And I'll dig out the poem and have it sent to you early tomorrow morning, Your Honor.'

TWO

'Political language . . . is designed to make lies sound truthful and murder respectable, and to give an appearance of solidity to pure wind.'

– George Orwell

'Turning and turning in the widening gyre
The falcon cannot hear the falconer;
Things fall apart; the center cannot hold;
Mere anarchy is loosed upon the world,
The blood-dimmed tide is loosed, and everywhere
The ceremony of innocence is drowned;
The best lack all conviction, while the worst
Are full of passionate intensity.'

– W.B. Yeats

'The only way to deal with an unfree world is to become so absolutely free that your very existence is an act of rebellion.'

– Albert Camus

It was now time for the lunch meeting that Judge Dee had told Yang in the morning to arrange in secrecy.

As always, Yang seemed to be on high alert – probably a bit too much – for his master's safety. In fact, Yang had been like that almost from the day he first became Judge Dee's servant, assistant and self-styled bodyguard as well. So Judge Dee was certain that Yang had made sure no one could, or would, hear anything about him meeting in secret to talk with the former Empress Wang's personal maid Ning.

Ning herself was too feeble to be able to find out anything about the mysterious invitation, or to uncover either Judge Dee's identity or Yang's.

Sitting in a private room, in a secluded, shaded restaurant that was some distance from the center of the capital, Judge Dee looked up to see Ning shuffling in, guided by Yang. She had a too pronounced stoop for her age, her steps unsteady, and a black veil hung over her face.

Yang himself had a similar veil covering his face. During this time of the Tang Empire, under the effective rule of Empress Wu, a large number of Arabian people traveled to the city of Chang'an. So a couple of veiled faces in the crowd would probably not appear to be conspicuous or suspicious.

Apparently, Ning was too sick to stay in the palace any more. A liability more than anything else, she looked like a shadow – or a skeleton – of her former self, though she was only in her late thirties. When she was safely inside the room, she pulled her veil back, revealing herself to be severely emaciated. Her disheveled hair was streaked with white, she had two front teeth missing, possibly owing to a bad fall or a vicious beating, and the corner of her left eye was continuously twitching. She could hardly stand up. There was a dazed, vacant look in her eyes, as if nothing mattered to her anymore – or was even visible to her.

Still, it was the fate of many palace girls to end up just like her. Having been touched – or even suspected of being touched – by the emperor, they were said to have been baptized with the divine dragon's dew and rain. Hence, they were no longer accessible to ordinary human beings. Otherwise, they could have been condemned as committing the worst profanity imaginable. They were helplessly doomed to stay pining and languishing in relentlessly imposed isolation for life.

It was a whispered yet open secret that an empress's personal maid, too, could have been taken by the emperor. Sometimes, she might have had to participate, like a submissive bedroom maid, in passionate sexual intercourse between the emperor and the empress, helping to push and pull in the midst of two panting, writhing, entwined bodies.

Ning had been allowed out of the royal palace probably because she was too sick. Besides, she failed to count exactly as a conventional palace girl.

One of Judge Dee's top priorities for this meeting with Ning was to fact-check the important, sensitive details about the empress in Luo Binwang's mighty poem-like statement 'Call to Arms'.

Ning alone was in a position to verify some of the essential information mentioned in the piece, which could then provide reliable clues for Judge Dee's investigation. So he'd had no option but to approach her in secret, even though it was a highly risky attempt, moving in a direction too sensitive to Empress Wu.

Judge Dee had heard plenty of sordid gossip about the empress's corrupt private life, and Luo's indignant 'Call to Arms' accused her of many infamous deeds in this respect. He could not neglect his duty, despite the risks, and ignore these rumors, which could prove vital to his investigation. He wanted to verify – or disprove – the points raised not merely by Luo Binwang but by her other accusers.

Judge Dee rose and helped Ning to slowly sit herself down at the table, on which eight small dishes of cold delicacies were already spread out. He picked up the silver wine kettle as he turned to Yang.

'You just wait outside the door, Yang. Don't let others enter. When the hot dishes are ready, you bring them in and serve them yourself. I do not want my talk with such an important guest to be disturbed.'

'Got you, Master. I will not step away.'

Dee then turned to Ning and poured the amber-colored rice wine into a dainty jade cup. 'Ning, I know you, and I know you have suffered a lot. It's so unfair to you.'

Ning took the cup from him with tremulous fingers. 'Who are you?'

'You don't have to worry about who I am. Not at all.' He continued with a reassuring smile, 'To put it another way – and excuse me for saying so – you've already fallen to rock bottom. There's nothing I can possibly do to hurt you any more than you've already been hurt. On the contrary, I will try my level best to do something good for you.'

'Really!' She drained the cup in one feeble gulp.

'This is just a simple meal in token of my sympathy for all

you have suffered,' he said, rising again to add more wine into her cup. 'I'm sorry, but I cannot stay and talk with you here for too long today. I'm leaving for a long trip tomorrow morning. So for now, please tell me about what really happened to your former mistress, Empress Wang – in as much detail as much as you can.'

Blinking her red-rimmed eyes in a daze for several minutes, Ning – sitting opposite Judge Dee – appeared still unable to grasp what was happening to her. She drained her second cup in another gulp. It was, Judge Dee supposed, another attempt to pull herself together. Or was she already an alcoholic?

She then managed to launch into a narration that was almost incoherent, and was frequently interrupted by coughing, hiccuping, drooling and sobbing. From time to time, her mind seemed to fail her, and at one point, she appeared to be lost in a total trance and sat there tongue-tied for no less than three or four minutes.

While listening to Ning's broken narration, Judge Dee could not help thinking of a poem titled 'The Outer Palace'. It was a sad and sentimental piece written by a well-known contemporary Tang poet named Yuan Zhen.

In the deserted outer palace,
the flowers bloom into a blaze
of solitary, scarlet splendor.
White-haired palace ladies
long deserted there, still
sit and talk languidly
about the late Tang emperor.

The vision presented an image that was so cruel, so heart-breaking to Judge Dee. In his reading, the elusive, fragmented, imagined memories of brief moments in the former lives of the palace ladies applied to Ning as well – in the company of the late emperor. And these brief moments seemed to provide the only meaning to her existence, both now and to the end of her life.

Indeed, what another poet says is so true.

If all time is eternally present
All time is unredeemable.

Judge Dee managed to put together a patchwork history of Empress Wu out of Ning's narration – distinguishable, although barely. According to Ning, Wu had been initially taken by the late Emperor Taizhong as nothing but a low-level palace lady. But it was an open secret that a palace lady could not say no to the emperor, in bed or anywhere else. And Emperor Taizhong had summoned Wu to his bedroom quite many times.

After the death of Emperor Taizhong, in accordance with convention, Wu was sent to a Daoist temple to be a nun, inaccessible to any other men for the rest of her life. In the Daoist temple, however, Wu soon started having secret rendezvous with Emperor Taizhong's son, the new Emperor Gaozhong. It could have been a huge scandal for him, as he had just ascended the throne and married Empress Wang, and he did not yet have his own power base consolidated. But rather than continue to meet Wu in secret, to the people's shock he soon officially summoned Wu into the palace. And, needless to say, into his bed.

Emperor Gaozhong lost no time promoting Wu to the top rank of imperial consorts, next only to Empress Wang. And Wu lost no time monopolizing the emperor's favor either. The emperor was so totally bewitched by Wu that he refused to take a step into Empress Wang's bedroom any more.

The next year, Wu gave birth to a female infant, who died mysteriously in its crib. To people's horror, evidence emerged suggesting that the cause of the death pointed toward brutal strangulation. Empress Wang had been seen visiting the infant's room shortly before the tragedy, and hence was a possible suspect.

Wu herself made the astonishing allegation that Empress Wang had murdered the infant out of insane jealousy. In corroboration, several eyewitnesses quickly rushed to the fore and testified about Empress Wang's stealthy visit to the baby's room that day.

Lacking a solid alibi, Empress Wang was unable to clear her name in the ensuing investigation, and Emperor Gaozhong was eventually led to believe that his wife had indeed killed the infant.

No credible information or evidence about the murder of Wu's daughter existed, however, and counter-theories and speculation began spreading like wild weeds. According to one popular theory, Wu herself had killed her own baby in order to implicate Empress Wang.

Throughout Ning's narration, she seemed to remain objective, without venturing to say anything about her opinion regarding the case. Did she think the former empress was a murderer, or that the current Empress Wu was the real murderer? If she had an opinion, she did not say.

As an experienced judge, Judge Dee knew he had to take into consideration that Ning had been crushed by the tyranny of Empress Wu. Ning dared not – or could not – speak truthfully of Empress Wu. Little wonder about that. The orthodox Confucianist officials tended to portray Empress Wu as an evil, power-hungry woman, cold-blooded about the people she wanted to get rid of. Even Judge Dee could not afford to take these counter-theories for granted.

Whatever the truth of the matter, Wu succeeded in removing Empress Wang from her royal position. The enraged emperor eventually deprived Wang of her title and replaced her with Wu, who became the next empress of the great Tang Empire.

Ning finished telling her tale, and Judge Dee silently added a further conclusion. For not too long after Wu became empress, her rival, the former Empress Wang, was murdered too. Another Tang Empire mystery that could not be solved, Judge Dee contemplated. Ning was not aware of the tragedy, as she'd been kept in isolation until about a month ago, and he chose not to break the news to her now. He knew it could prove to be too much of a shock.

Judge Dee drained his cup with a long sigh and watched despondently as Ning shuffled out of the room with the help of Yang, her face veiled again, her body tremulous like a black raven in the cold wind.

Incredibly, Dee thought, Ning's patchwork account largely verified Luo Binwang's account of Empress Wu's crimes in his 'Call to Arms'.

* * *

Three or four hours later, Judge Dee invited a group of poets to dinner at a quiet, willow-shaded hostel located on the outskirts of the Chang'an capital.

It happened also to be on the way to the first stop he had decided to take for his investigation, so it was natural for him to choose the hostel for the night. After all, he was an old man, too worn out to travel overnight.

Judge Dee had arranged the dinner party for the purpose of gathering and sorting through more information about the vanished Luo. All five of the poets he'd invited were renowned for their work, though they were not as well known as Jiong Yang or Luo Binwang.

Now, the poets had all arrived at the hostel, and they gathered together for the meal. A light dinner was already laid out on the round table in the center of the private dining room for them.

Judge Dee stood up, cleared his throat, raised a cup and started his prepared speech.

'Welcome to the hostel this evening. As you may have already heard, Her Majesty has entrusted me with the mission of finding the missing Luo Binwang. As an aged, overwhelmed official, I know little about a poet like him. You are all well-known poets, and you must have met and talked with Luo. Therefore, anything you can tell me tonight about Luo will prove to be a tremendous help to me.'

'You're such a brilliant, resourceful judge, Your Honor,' the poet surnamed Shangguan responded immediately. 'Who else is there that Her Majesty can trust like you? For others, it may take months or even longer to get any clues regarding a missing person like Luo. For you, however, gathering evidence is a piece of cake. You have the typical sixth sense that is characteristic of a great poet and a resourceful judge.'

'No, no, it's far from being that easy, I tell you,' Judge Dee said. 'Nor am I a poet like all of you here. It's true I once dreamed of a career as a poet in my younger days, but soon I knew better. And in the meantime, Her Majesty just kept giving me one assignment after another, you know – assignments that have nothing to do with poetry, and thus I have no time for poetry.

As a matter of fact, I have not written a single readable poem for years.

'I've invited you all here this evening in the hope that you may help by giving me a comprehensive background picture of Luo. All of you are well-known poets, and so must have been in close contact with Luo in the past. Anything – everything – from you will contribute to the success of the investigation. Particularly your knowledge about the possible places Luo might be hiding in right at this moment.'

'The ringleader of the rebellion, General Xu himself, was killed in the last battle fought by the Wuding River,' Shangguan replied, the red wine in his white jade cup rippling like blood in the candlelight. 'I don't think an old bookworm like Luo Binwang could have possibly escaped alive, Your Honor.'

'I have suggested a similar scenario to Her Majesty, but she's so anxious to gather talents around her that she will not listen to me,' Judge Dee said, shaking his head. 'She is adamant that until his body is discovered – either on the battlefield or elsewhere – I have to continue investigating.'

Perhaps, as in the old Chinese saying, it takes coincidences to make a story. Their discussion was interrupted by a light knock on the door of the private dining room. The opening door framed a middle-aged official surnamed Yuwen. Agricultural Minister Yuwen was said to have an ambiguous political stance between the two rival factions at the court: the Li group, which was composed of loyalists to the late emperor's family, and the Wu group, which was composed of loyalists to the empress's family. Perhaps like Judge Dee himself, in spite of his serving in a fairly high-ranking position under the empress, Yuwen was seen by a number of other scholars as an orthodox Confucianist in his own way.

Judge Dee did not recollect that he had put Minister Yuwen's name on the invitation list for this dinner, so he was more than a little surprised at his unexpected guest. It was unconventional for a minister like Yuwen to join with other guests – if not invited – to discuss something like the Luo case. A considerable number of low-ranking officials under Minister Yuwen could have easily provided him with information about the progress of the Luo Binwang case if he wished.

As a result, Judge Dee could not help thinking: would it be possible that Empress Wu had sent Minister Yuwen over for surveillance of the dinner tonight?

Judge Dee's latest proposal at the court to the empress had been commonly seen as a deliberate effort to persuade Wu not to change the dynasty of the Li family to that of the Wu family. They both knew that only too well. In fact, it was entirely possible that the case of Luo's disappearance had been assigned to him by the empress as part of a conspiracy to push him out of the capital. It could be a calculated move by Her Majesty to remove an obstacle in her path to consolidating her absolute power over the Tang Empire.

'Her Majesty wants me to take on this new job as soon as possible, so I'm leaving early tomorrow morning,' Judge Dee said. 'I'm just asking some poet-friends over for a cup before I leave. Hopefully, they may also be able to tell me something about Luo.'

'The Luo case is indeed becoming a sensational one, involving not only a celebrated poet but a number of well-known men of letters too, Your Honor,' Minister Yuwen said, nodding his head gravely. 'And people are talking about it as a case symbolic of the mess under Her Majesty in today's empire. In the interests of maintaining political stability for the empire, it is crucial that there is a quick conclusion to the case. Your work will be vital.'

If he had been sent by the empress, Minister Yuwen would have been kept well informed of Judge Dee's whereabouts. So it was little wonder, after all, that he was here, Judge Dee thought.

'You surely have a point, Minister Yuwen. It is indeed a politically significant case. I'll see what I can do, but I don't have any clues for the moment, let alone any theories.'

'I've heard that a large-scale search for Luo Binwang has yielded no results,' Yuwen said, seating himself in an unoccupied chair beside Judge Dee. 'So I will share what I know about Luo myself. Years ago, I happened to be taking the state-level civil service examination with Luo. That year, we stayed at the same hostel in the capital, waiting for the result. I came out successful, and he failed, even though he wrote better poems than I. He is a very proud man in his way, as you may know.

'You certainly could say it was not fair to Luo. I have since paid continuous attention to him – long before the outbreak of the rebellion. He's a great poet, no question about it. In my opinion, he's qualified to rank number one of the "Four Most Excellent Poets" of our time.'

Yuwen then began to share more recent information with Judge Dee and others at the table.

'According to gossip, Luo was said to be seen alive, although severely wounded, after the rebellion's final battle fought by the Wuding River. Some claimed Luo was seen in a small village near the battlefield. Some maintained it was in a high-end brothel. Others insisted it was at a Buddhist temple. But none of the rumors seemed to be that reliable. The distance between these places appears to be far too great for Luo to have moved between them all in such a short space of time. Unless Luo has wings, which is ridiculous.'

'Yes, for a severely wounded old man, Luo would not have been capable of venturing too far,' the poet surnamed Zhou cut in. 'It's totally out of the question.'

'In any case, soldiers must have combed through all those areas,' said Ouyang stubbornly, a poet known for his *Ci*-style work. 'You can never tell where one may choose to hide. He could have been staying invisible in the most obvious places. Zhuang Zi has a famous saying frequently quoted by people, generation after generation: "A great recluse hides himself in the very center of the city."'

'What about his old home?' said another poet surnamed Wei.

'You are familiar with his old home, Wei?'

'I came from a county just a couple of miles from his. So I have heard a thing or two about him. His parents passed away long ago, and he has only one younger sister staying in their old home. He broke contact with her years ago because she insisted he should receive no share of what his parents had left behind. She complained that he had stayed away from home for a long time, failing to take care of their parents. She said he was selfish, egocentric and contemptuous of other people.'

'But he participated in the civil service examination many times,' Judge Dee said. 'All the preparations, travel and expenses . . . It's little wonder that he could not afford to stay at home for a long period.'

'His old home is too far away from the Wuding River battlefield, though,' Shangguan chimed in. 'And it would have been too dangerous for him to travel all the way back there when the fight was over.'

'I've read a poem allegedly written by Luo before he joined the rebellion's army,' Minister Yuwen said, cutting in again. 'There're different stories about the poem. Naturally, the stories are not that reliable, I have to say, and the authorship of the poem may be a bit questionable too. But the mood of the poem fits well with Luo. Here it is, and I read it out for all of you. The title is "Seeing off a friend by Yi River":

'Here, the brave assassin Jin Ke
bid farewell to his lord Prince Yan,
his hair bristling with indignation.
All the heroic and the gallant deeds
of the past long gone, the water
of the Yi River remains bone-chilling.'

'If it's true, it becomes Luo well,' Judge Dee said. 'The poem is about a courageous man, Jin Ke. On the eve of the first emperor of the Qin Empire conquering China, Jin Ke set out to assassinate him. Jin Ke knew it was an impossible mission for him to assassinate the mighty emperor. Nevertheless, as it appeared to him, it was the right thing for him to do. So, once he had bid farewell to his friends and sung a song about the cold water in the Yi River, he set out to do it. He failed in the assassination attempt, but even today people admire his courage. You could probably say Luo also bid a tragic farewell himself in that poem.'

'Yes, the choice of the intertextual leitmotif speaks volumes about the poem. A heroic elegy not just for Jin Ke, but for Luo too,' Yuwen concurred moodily, 'before he set out for that last, fatal attempt of his. The river surely marked a point of no return for him. It was sort of his swan song.'

'Luo knew that only too well,' Zhou said, 'but he still wanted to join the rebellion.'

The poem was passed around the people sitting at the dinner table. Someone took in a sharp breath, as if he were about to speak, but no one said anything more in response.

After all, such a discussion could be a serious political taboo. As in the Chinese proverb, walls have ears.

Especially with the uninvited Minister Yuwen sitting among the poets at the table. There was not even a wall.

Later, in his hostel room, Judge Dee combed and re-combed his white-streaked beard with two fingers, lost in thought.

The discussion with the five poets in the hostel restaurant had hardly yielded anything relevant or fruitful to the investigation, and Judge Dee remained disturbed by the surprising visit made by Minister Yuwen.

Could it have been a not-too-subtle hint that the empress was keeping all of them under surveillance, so they'd better behave themselves? At the same time, it was also possible that Her Majesty had just wanted to provide Dee with all the information available concerning the investigation, including Luo's poem about Jin Ke, and had been deadly serious from the outset about him actually finding Luo.

Or could it be possible that there was something else behind it? Something Her Majesty did not want Judge Dee to know about the investigation into the missing poet. Some kind of hidden agenda.

Still lost in thought, watching the flickering candlelight by the western window of the hostel room, Judge Dee tried not to dwell too much on the politics behind the case.

It looked as though it was going to rain soon. A small pool in the back of the hostel appeared to be swelling with the old memories of those bygone days. A couple of half-forgotten lines came back to his mind in the somberness of the room.

A candle trembling against the night rain,
you travel across rivers and lakes, year after year . . .

The night appeared to be so quiet and peaceful, far away from the sordid politics at the imperial court. Judge Dee turned to stare absentmindedly at a blurred reflection of his worn-out self in the bronze mirror. He knew he would not be able to fall asleep any time soon. It was perhaps just another sign of the onset of old age, he supposed.

It was growing surreally dark outside the time-yellowed paper window, though, and Dee could hear a dog barking like crazy in the pitch-black distance.

Finally, a faint drowsiness was beginning to creep over him, suggesting he might finally be ready to go to bed, when he heard an unexpected light knock on the door.

In came Yang, bringing a wet message of the night rain.

Taking a gulp from the cup of hot tea Judge Dee offered him, Yang launched into a report of the new information he had gathered concerning the Luo case. It was not much, he said, not that relevant, yet there was a lot of new salacious material regarding the empress. This gossip seemed to Dee to be yet more of the particularly serious repercussions of Luo's 'Call to Arms'.

According to the scurrilous gossip Yang had gleaned, the empress was currently enraptured with her discovery of a virile monk named Xue Huaiyi, who was said to boast an enormous penis – as thick, long and hard as a virile man's arm.

During the first night they had passionate sex in the royal palace, she climaxed repeatedly, trembling violently, flushing all over . . .

In the aftermath of the white clouds turning into hot rain between the two naked, sweat-glistening bodies, Xue was said to have quoted verbatim the empress's rapturous exclamation after their sordid sex in a secret diary: 'Finally, I have lived and died once as a woman.'

And possibly he had written a lot more in this diary too . . .

The empress knew better, though, than to get lost for too long in sexual passion. While she kept showering gifts and favors upon the monk Xue, so the gossip went, she also managed to keep him at a certain distance from things at the court.

Judge Dee thought he had already heard something about this

scandal. It was disconcerting, but he did not see its immediate relevance to the investigation.

And, needless to say, high-ranking officials like Judge Dee knew better than to confront the infamous monk. As in the old saying: if you plan to beat a dog, you must first take the owner of the dog into consideration.

'But what about Luo Binwang?' Judge Dee asked, switching the topic after a short pause. 'Anything new you have learned about him?'

'No, not anything concrete, Your Honor. Nothing but unreliable gossip and speculation. According to one explanation, which seems plausible, it is said that Luo was thrown into prison not for slandering Empress Wu but because he refused to write a poem in praise of her. Regardless of the truth, though, that would have happened long before the disastrous rebellion led by General Xu.'

'Gossip is not reliable, not at all. I cannot agree more with you, Yang. Her Majesty surely knows better than to imprison a poet for refusing to write a poem.'

'People also say that Luo wrote a poem in prison, comparing himself to a fly or some such insect.'

'Yes, that may be true. "Ode to a Cicada in Prison." Wonderful personification.'

Yang didn't reply; he was out of his element engaging in the interpretation of poetry, Judge Dee knew.

After Yang had left his hostel room, Judge Dee stepped out into the courtyard, standing alone in the wind and the darkness.

He had a vague feeling that there was something he'd missed in the midst of all the possible pieces of a gigantic puzzle, but for the moment he was unable to put his finger on it.

Outside, the night watchman was making another round, beating the wooden knocker in a monotonous pattern against the night and retreating further into the darkness.

There was such a lot of work he would have to do, Judge Dee knew, before he could get anywhere in the investigation. Work for which he had neither the time nor the final say – which belonged to Empress Wu alone.

Judge Dee felt that, all of a sudden, he had become a string-controlled shadow puppet, gesticulating on the cloth screen, speaking not in his voice but in accordance with the role of a character moving on the dimly lit stage.

THREE

'I only go out to get me a fresh appetite for being alone.'
– Lord Byron

'To see a world in a grain of sand
And a heaven in a wild flower,
Hold infinity in the palm of your hand,
And eternity in an hour.'

– William Blake

'A man is never happy, but spends his whole life in striving after something that he thinks will make him so; he seldom attains his goal, and when he does, it is only to be disappointed; he is mostly shipwrecked in the end, and comes into harbor with mast and rigging gone. And then, it is all one whether he is happy or miserable; for his life was never anything more than a present moment always vanishing; and now it is over.'
– Arthur Schopenhauer

The next morning broke with a messenger galloping over in a great hurry from Jiong. Judge Dee hurried out to meet him. The rider was still panting, out of breath, and carried two copies of Luo's poems supposedly written for the fishing girl, along with a letter from Jiong himself:

'These are the poems attributed to Luo Binwang which were allegedly written for the fishing girl I told you about. The authorship of the second piece may be open to question, and some of the background information could be nothing but hearsay. But I have checked through a list of Luo's poems made by a little-known critic. These two poems were written in the same period, though the critic also points out the stylistic differences between them.

'Anyway, Luo's stay on the boat with the fishing girl has been confirmed. For a short while, either before or after he was thrown into prison.

'According to the critic, the fishing girl in question was also described as a capable chef, specializing in catching the fish or shrimp live out of the river water and cooking it on the boat there and then. It is little wonder that men of letters flocked to the special boat, not just for the delicious food, but also for the delicious girl bustling around the fish, her body still wet from the river, the scanty clothes clinging to her body and hugging her curves. Indeed, such a moment is worth thousands of gold coins.

'It was also said, however, that she knew how to keep the necessary distance from those men flirting around her like insistent butterflies, and that she behaved properly, on the whole, as the chef and sampan owner.

'Best luck for your trip, Your Honor!'

But that morning did not turn out to be an auspicious one for Judge Dee.

Shortly afterward, another messenger hurried over. He was one of Yang's shady connections, surnamed Liao, and he came to report the death of Ning, the former Empress Wang's personal maid. Ning had been found hanging on a tall date tree in a deserted courtyard. According to Liao, the rigor of the body suggested that Ning could have hanged herself there around midnight.

One thing struck Judge Dee as odd. Liao claimed that he could not see any signs of a chair or ladder near her cold, stiff body at the scene of her apparent suicide. Could she have jumped up from the ground so high as to reach her head into the dangling loop overhead?

No, Judge Dee did not think so, either, and the sickly Ning had no strength to do the job by herself, even with a ladder. She could not even have walked in and out of the restaurant the previous day without Yang's support, her legs wobbling all the time, he recalled with the sensation of something like a bucket of ice water pouring down his spine.

If she hadn't taken her own life, had Ning been murdered and the suicide scene clumsily fabricated?

Then Judge Dee shivered again at an unexpected, newly emerging possibility. An owl hooted eerily in the small woods near the hostel, as if echoing from an ancient horror story.

Could the murder have been caused – directly or not – by his meeting with Ning the previous day? The state surveillance of the Tang Empire could be so horribly effective. Empress Wu had numerous secret agents working hectically under her like ants before the arrival of heavy rain. Ning too must have been surveilled and shadowed all the time—

Similarly, Minister Yuwen's surprising visit to the party of the poets had been plotted by the empress for the same purpose: to put the investigator Judge Dee under constant secret surveillance.

An ancient saying came into Judge Dee's mind, and he paraphrased it then and there for the occasion. 'I did not kill Ning, but she died because of me.' The judge was overwhelmed by a huge wave of sadness. It was true that he had to leave today. If he did not do so, the far-reaching net of surveillance would catch him in no time. But he still had to look into the death of Ning.

'Yang,' Judge Dee said, turning to his servant, 'tell your connection Liao to continue looking into the death of Ning. Anything and everything suspicious shortly before her death? Who had contacted her? She had lost two of her front teeth. Could she have suffered vicious beatings or torture? Were there any palace ladies who were a friend to her?'

'I'll carry out your order, Master. Before we set out for the trip?'

'Yes, we have to leave today. Give Liao a handsome retainer fee, and ask him not to spare any cost or to say anything about it to others.'

'So where are we going today, Master?' Yang asked as he returned after quite some time to the side of the carriage. It startled Judge Dee out of his dark, drowsy thoughts.

'Um, let's go to the Wuding River first,' he decided.

'Why, Master?'

'That's where the last battle was fought between the rebellious and royal armies . . . and also where Luo was reported missing,' Judge Dee added after a short pause. 'According to the latest information provided by the empress last night, Luo had stayed there previously with a local herbal doctor surnamed Hua, who treated him for a minor wound sustained in an earlier battle.'

'The trip could take more than one day, possibly two days, Master.'

'But do we have any choice?' Judge Dee asked, shaking his head with resignation before he went on. 'Can we manage to speed up our journey – travel there as fast as possible?'

'I'll try my best, Master, but more likely than not, we will not be able to reach Wuding River until tomorrow.' Then, handing over something like an envelope, Yang hurriedly added, 'Here is something for you.'

'What's that?'

'Liao's first report.'

'This is just a preliminary report, Your Honor, written in a great hurry. Yang insists on it, saying you're leaving to pursue the investigation in other cities. So it is a combination of something I may have already told Yang, but a bit more detailed – plus something I have *not* yet told Yang.

'Regarding Ning, I came to notice her because she moved into the area under the control of our Green Bamboo Group. Control only in a dark way, needless to say, but our group is not unconnected with the government authorities, you know. She moved over from a mysterious place, all by herself. What's more, she appeared to have been put under secret state surveillance. For a sickly, harmless, middle-aged woman like Ning, why all the bother?

'We knew nothing about her background, but we knew better than to get involved. We just kept an eye on her. She hardly mixed with her neighbors. And she seldom came out, except for essential grocery shopping.

'Early this morning, one of the younger brothers in our group reported that he had heard some strange noises in her deserted back courtyard. So he and I hurried over there for a sneak view.

To our horror, we saw Ning hanged on the withered pagoda tree. Her tongue was sticking out, her hair was disheveled, her body totally rigid. At a rough estimate, the time of death could be shortly after midnight. It's just our guess, of course.

'Yang may have told you about one thing suspicious at the scene of her death. We did not find a ladder or a tall chair underneath her lifeless body. It's hard to imagine she actually had the strength to jump into the loop dangling high on the tree.

'And then we checked into her meagerly furnished room. There were no signs of her putting up a struggle there. The room had been ransacked, however, with everything turned upside down. That, too, beat us. Apparently, she was not someone with enough money to warrant a possible murder at midnight. Nor was Ning a woman who could read or write. We happened to know that because she had once been asked to fill out the registration in the neighborhood, and she told us she was illiterate . . .'

The part about Ning's mysterious arrival at an area under the control of the Green Bamboo Group – or Green Bamboo Gang – was no mystery to Judge Dee. Driven out of the palace, she had to be placed somewhere. What struck the judge as particularly suspicious was the fact that the murderer, either before or after the murder, did a thorough search of her place. It was not for money; Liao had ruled out that possibility. For something left by the former Empress Wang? Judge Dee ruled that out too. When Ning was driven out of the palace, she must have been searched and re-searched from head to toe. For something related to Ning's meeting with the judge? Dee could not rule it out, though he was bamboozled about it.

'I don't know whether this information will be of help to your investigation. Anyway, I'll keep you posted with anything new. It's such a great honor for you to entrust me with the job. How can I not exert myself like a dog, like a horse, Your Honor!'

Yang, sitting in the front of the carriage again, raised the whip, ready to crack it. It was already almost lunchtime.

'So here we are, at the beginning of our investigation. A long, long trip indeed, Master.'

As the carriage started rolling out, Judge Dee felt increasingly drowsy in spite of his effort to concentrate on the Luo case. He lifted the carriage curtain a little to see outside. The scene still appeared to be familiar.

Out of the capital, the road then became uneven. Thanks to the considerate, thoughtful Yang, who had placed several soft cotton-padded cushions in the carriage for his master, Judge Dee was not jolted too badly. And there was an extra-soft, damask-covered pillow as well.

The scenes flashing past outside now appeared to the judge to be dull, dispirited. The carriage wheels rolled on with a mechanical, monotonous hum. Eventually, he could not help sinking into sleep, slipping in and out of weird dreams.

Several characters seemed to be drifting past on a dimly lit gigantic stage. Empress Wu, Emperor Gaozhong, the former Empress Wang, Luo Binwang, Ning . . . these, plus many others, kept popping in and out of the fragmented dream, insubstantial yet so real and intense. After all, men and women are but such stuff as dreams are made of, including Judge Dee himself.

FOUR

'When you see millions of the mouthless dead
Across your dreams in pale battalions go,
Say not soft things as other men have said,
That you'll remember. For you need not so . . .'

– Charles Sorley

'I have always thought the actions of men the best interpreters of their thoughts.'

– John Locke

'Life is a sum of all your choices. So, what are you doing today?'

– Albert Camus

It was almost the afternoon of the second day when the travel-weary master and servant reached their destination, with the view of the Wuding River rolling to the distant horizon.

A couple of water birds could be seen frolicking tirelessly over the river's surface, their white wings flashing energetically under the golden light, as if eager in their attempt to catch something out of the shimmering ripples.

Indeed, it had been such a long journey. And such a long river too. Judge Dee had no idea, however, as to where exactly the last battle in question had been fought. So he decided to check into a nearby hostel first. Yang agreed, more than readily.

Once he had the information about the location of the battlefield from the hostel's front desk, Judge Dee wanted to go there straight away to present an offering to those who had died in the battles near the Wuding River. He saw it as the responsibility of a high-ranking government official in his position.

He was aware of a tragic irony in Tang history. Seven or eight years earlier, another bloody battle had been fought by the river, between barbarian aggressors and the grand Tang royal army. The recent battle had been equally ferocious and cruel, if not more so. According to unofficial statistics, far more people had died in General Xu's crushed rebellion than in that earlier battle.

The coincidence triggered Judge Dee's memory about a touching poem composed by a contemporary poet Chen Tao, who was also known for his focus on the inhumanity of wars.

Pledged to wipe out the Huns,
they fought without any thoughts
for themselves, and then died,
all of them, five thousand sable-clad warriors,
lost in the dust of the North.

Alas, the white bones scattered there
by the faraway Wuding River
still come in spring to haunt women's dreams,
in the shapes of their dead lovers.

At the new battlefield, Judge Dee was more than shocked at the sight of white bones sticking out like accusing fingers, black ravens screeching, circling overhead, ready to pounce on the decaying carcasses in the field.

A tiny yellow flower was blossoming in an empty human eye socket, which still seemed to be scanning the field, the flower swaying in the mournful wind that swept over the wasteland.

Were these wars and battles justified?

Politicians would surely say yes, of course, arguing with sticky saliva frothing around their mouths, veins stretching out like earthworms on their foreheads. They believed that they had no choice. The interest and welfare of the Han nationality could not tolerate any harm. Nor could the so-called political stability under the rein of the great Empress Wu.

But what about the Huns in the poem? And what about their surviving wives and families after the battles? The heart-breaking scene happened to the Huns too, as so sensationally depicted in the poem by Chen Tao.

Even more immediately, what about the dead and wounded in this new battlefield, which was still littered with bodies, decaying under Judge Dee's very eyes? After all, that bloody battle was fought among the Han people.

According to Luo Binwang in the 'Call to Arms', the war was perfectly justified. And the same could be argued just as passionately from Empress Wu's side.

Mencius, a Confucian scholar considered in imperial China to be second only to Confucius himself in philosophical status, put it very well: 'During the long, long Spring and Autumn period, there were no just or justified wars.'

That was probably why Mencius had to rank after Confucius in China.

Mencius also said, 'People are the most important, the welfare of the state next, and the emperor least of all.' Naturally, the emperors did not like Mencius.

For Judge Dee, another quote from Mencius, which had served him as a key principle during his official career so far, came flashing through his mind again.

If you don't stand upright, you cannot see the way ahead.

To Judge Dee's surprise, the moment he arrived back at the fairly comfortable hostel and stepped inside, the local mayor surnamed Zhuang hurried over in a vermilion official sedan chair.

As it turned out, Mayor Zhuang had been one of the successful candidates at the capital-level civil service examination more than a decade ago. It was an event that just so happened to have been supervised by the high-ranking Minister Dee. So Mayor Zhuang had come to claim himself as a disciple of Judge Dee's.

'Welcome, Your Honor,' Mayor Zhuang said, all smiles. 'I've just prepared a light meal to wash the dust of the long trip from my distinguished mentor. It is nothing but a token of my sincere gratitude.'

Following the mayor, Zhuang's two servants took cold and hot dishes out of the food baskets they were carrying and spread them out on a small table in Judge Dee's hostel room. They also placed on the table a dainty silver wine kettle, full of nicely warmed, amber-colored sticky rice wine.

Strictly speaking, Mayor Zhuang could not be counted as a student of Judge Dee's, who had just happened to be the high-ranking official in charge of the capital civil service examination that year. Judge Dee would not have met any of the candidates in person, including Mayor Zhuang. He merely gave grades to their papers in a separate room, unapproachable, unknown to the candidates. But it was conventional for successful candidates – grateful for the high grades they had obtained – to acknowledge their examiner as their mentor.

It might be just as well, though, Judge Dee thought. He had been exhausted by the trip. Although he had been seated all the way, supported by those soft cushions Yang had placed in the carriage, he still felt as if his old bones had been shaken out of their joints. Not to mention the fact that Yang had been driving the carriage all the time, and the tireless assistant definitely needed a break as well.

More importantly, Mayor Zhuang might be able to tell him something more about Luo's possible whereabouts. Since Zhuang looked up to Judge Dee not only as a superior official but also as his mentor, it would be a matter of course that the mayor would go out of his way to help.

And so it soon proved.

'I was so honored to have been your student, Your Honor,' Mayor Zhuang said respectfully with another bow. 'I've only just heard that you would be arriving at the Wuding River today, as part of your investigation into the disappearance of Luo Binwang. But I have already started planning what I, one of your most humble students, could possibly do for you.'

Busy piling up the delicacies on Judge Dee's plate on the small table, Mayor Zhuang lost no time in briefing his mentor about the ferocious battle that had been fought by the Wuding River not too long ago, and sharing all the information he knew concerning Luo Binwang, the missing person in question.

'According to the information we have so far collected, Your Honor, Luo was reported missing in the last battle fought here by the rebellious army. Before that battle, Xu's troops had gathered here for about a month or so. During their stay, nobody but a local herbal doctor surnamed Hua came into close contact with Luo. Luo had sustained a minor wound in an earlier battle, and Doctor Hua was responsible for taking care of Luo's wound in his small hut. With Hua's effective herbal prescriptions and acupuncture treatments, Luo was said to have enjoyed an amazingly speedy recovery. The two seemed to have been getting along pretty well, according to the neighbors there, talking and discussing a lot with each other.

'Hua had taken part in the civil service examinations in his twenties and thirties but was not successful. So he became an herbal doctor here, though he remained a passionate reader of poetry and a huge fan of Luo's poems. It was understandable that Hua did his level best to take care of Luo. Before rejoining the rebellious troops seven or eight days prior to the last battle, Luo was said to have written a poem for Hua in appreciation of his help.

'Consequently, local people began speculating about the possibility that, after the annihilation of General Xu's army in the battle by the Wuding River, Hua could have helped Luo into hiding somewhere nearby. Naturally, Hua has been repeatedly interrogated, and his hut searched and re-searched, with everything turned upside down. In reality, the whole area, not just Hua's hut, has been combed and re-combed, both by local runners and the secret police specially dispatched from above. In spite of all their efforts, though, they drew a blank. I know all this because our local police joined in the thorough search for Luo Binwang.'

Although Luo's close connection to the local herbal doctor, Hua, was not exactly news to Judge Dee, the fact that the secret police had thoroughly combed the area and found nothing did not come as a surprise to him. While he could not afford to completely rule out the theory Mayor Zhuang was talking about, it seemed highly unlikely to the experienced Judge Dee.

Besides, in the Tang dynasty, most ordinary people chose to believe wholeheartedly in an emperor or an empress, who was endowed with what was commonly accepted to be a divine mandate to rule over the country. To them, it did not really matter who exactly was sitting on the splendid throne, especially at a time like this when the country happened to be enjoying a relatively peaceful and prosperous period in its history. If Luo was hiding nearby, someone would have noticed him, and the news of the dangerous poet's whereabouts would have spread.

'It was such a cruel battle indeed,' Zhuang went on, shaking his head like a rattle drum. 'The river water was dyed red with blood. For a month or so, no one wanted to taste the fish or shrimp caught in the stinking, scarlet liquid.'

'So local fishing people must have suffered a huge loss of income?' Judge Dee inquired.

'Fortunately, the river no longer smells so horrible, Your Honor.'

'A different question for you now, Zhuang. Do you happen to know the herbal doctor surnamed Hua well?'

'You're asking because of his connection with Luo Binwang?'

'That's right,' Judge Dee replied.

'In fact, some people from the capital recently contacted me again, asking about Doctor Hua.'

'Who were those people?'

'The secret police, I guess. They must have had a direct order from the very top in the Forbidden City.'

'I see,' Judge Dee said, even though he still did not see why Empress Wu had set so much store by finding Luo. Now that the uprising had been firmly defeated, what harm could an old, wounded poet do?

Mayor Zhuang then launched into a more detailed background report about Hua, and about the herbal doctor's relationship with Luo. It did not seem to contain anything new or relevant to what he'd already spoken about, though. And if the secret police had already interrogated Dr Hua and repeatedly searched his hut, but found nothing, surely the man had nothing to hide? Dee could not understand their continued interest in him.

'In other words,' Judge Dee said reflectively at the conclusion of Zhuang's report, 'there seemed to be nothing particularly suspicious about the relationship between Luo and Hua.'

'Nothing. If anything aroused suspicion, it must just be that the two of them had talked quite a lot – Luo and Hua, I mean. But that may not be considered surprising. Hua had participated in the civil service examination – several times – without success. Luo had succeeded, but not until he was in his late forties. So they might have shared some common experiences and topics.'

FIVE

'The real voyage of discovery consists not in seeking new landscapes, but in having new eyes.'

– Marcel Proust

'What we think or what we know or what we believe is in the end of little consequence. The only thing of consequence is what we do.'

– John Ruskin

'Do not blame Caesar, blame the people of Rome who have so enthusiastically acclaimed and adored him and rejoiced in their loss of freedom and danced in his path and gave him triumphal processions. Blame the people who hail him when he speaks in the Forum of the "new, wonderful good society" which shall now be Rome, interpreted to mean "more money, more ease, more security, more living fatly at the expense of the industrious".'

– Marcus Tullius Cicero

Early the next morning, Judge Dee approached Dr Hua's hut with slow steps. As he chewed a betel nut, he cudgeled his brains, thinking and re-thinking about what plausible excuse he should give for the unannounced visit to the herbal doctor.

A splendid pheasant flashed up from a patch of the roadside bushes, dazzling in the sunlight, as Judge Dee moved into view of the wooden hut in question. From a distance, he could see the hut was discolored and ramshackle, constructed of pinewood, with several large pieces of bark peeling from its outside walls. It was located close to the small, shady woods. He could hear a faint gurgling sound from somewhere nearby, so he deduced there was probably a tiny stream behind it.

At closer range, he was able to discern the black holes here and there in its thatch roof, like footnotes about the poverty of its inhabitant. There were a couple of tiny holes in the time-yellowed paper window as well. It would be far from a pleasant experience for people to stay there on rainy days.

After knocking on the door once, and then again, yet getting no response, Judge Dee gingerly pushed it open.

He could see a bamboo basket lying on the ground inside the threshold, containing a variety of fresh herbs, still lushly green with dewdrops visible on the fresh leaves. They could have been collected earlier in the morning. By the side of the basket, he noticed something else – like a spade but smaller, with a different-shaped head. Quite possibly, it was a tool specially designed for the purpose of digging and gathering herbs in the high mountains. A pair of wet-mud-covered straw sandals lay nearby, further anchoring Judge Dee's impression of the impoverishment of the hut's owner.

For a moment, Judge Dee could not help recalling several idyllic lines written by another contemporary poet named Jia Dao. He then suddenly felt unsure about the authorship. It could be just another sign of his impending old age, and he heaved a sigh at being so forgetful, and sentimental too.

I inquire of a young boy servant
standing under a pine tree.
'My master is away,' he said,
'collecting medical herbs,
somewhere secluded in the mountains,
deep in the white clouds—
but about exactly where? Um,
I cannot really tell.'

It was nothing but a Daoist poetic vision. In the real world, a herbal doctor like Hua, living in the mountainous countryside, had to struggle hard for survival. To say the least, Hua did not have 'a young boy servant' waiting around for him.

What was worse, Hua must have been ruthlessly, repeatedly interrogated about Luo, and eventually uprooted into an omnipresent, omnipotent basket of government surveillance. There was no possibility of his escaping – as in the poetic fantasy – into the peaceful, white-cloud-mantled mountains.

Judge Dee was trying to suppress another long sigh, shaking his head, when Hua stepped into the room. He was a man who pretty much looked his age, his temples silver-streaked and his brow deep-lined. Wearing a homespun long gray gown, and a pair of dry straw sandals, Hua hurried over to meet Judge Dee and made a respectful bow still at a distance. The long gown, usually worn by intellectuals, somehow contributed to Judge Dee's impression of him being an experienced, learned doctor.

Judge Dee offered Dr Hua his business card.

'Your visit really brightens up my humble abode, Your Honor,' Hua said, carefully taking the card from his hand. 'Wow, Judge Dee? Indeed, it's such an honor for an obscure country bumpkin like me.'

'We both study Confucian classics, Doctor Hua. So what's the difference between us? You are also an experienced medical doctor. According to an ancient saying, one should be either a good politician or a good doctor. In unstable times like ours, a politician's scheme might work for the current moment, but it could also turn out to be a huge disaster in disguise. On the other hand, being a good doctor is different: you save so many lives. In fact, I wish I, too, could serve as a life-saving doctor like you.'

'You flatter me too much, Your Honor. I have heard of people saying a lot of things about you – mostly good.' Hua came straight to the point. 'To be honest, I know little about politics, and I'm not in a position to judge. Nonetheless, I believe you're an insightful statesman of integrity in your own way, resourceful and far-sighted in terms of seeing the bigger picture with regard to the welfare of the whole empire. I've been particularly impressed by your courageous suggestion to the empress in the court. I mean, of course, the suggestion about keeping the Lis in line for the smooth succession to the throne. It's all for the welfare of the Tang Empire and the Tang people, I understand. So please go ahead with whatever questions you want to ask me. I'll try my best to answer.'

'I think I got your point, and I thank you so much, Doctor

Hua. It's understandable what some people might have said about me, both good and bad. Let me tell you one thing that recently happened to me. Just before I set out for this trip, I called on my sister-in-law. When I was still a young boy, she married my elder brother. She took very good care of me for years, even after my elder brother passed away in an accident, until the time I succeeded in the civil service examination and obtained an official position. It's just like in the old Chinese saying: a kind elder sister-in-law could have been like a mother. I've been deeply beholden to her all these years, and she knows that. But that day she gave me such a harsh dressing down.

'"You're bringing shame to this door, Renjie, and to our family name of Dee. You actually have the nerve to grovel at the feet of that lascivious bitch of a woman, and to bark like a mad dog on her behalf, trying to hunt Luo Binwang down. Luo Binwang did the right and proper thing when he composed his powerful 'Call to Arms'. All of the details in the declaration are true. He did nothing wrong."

'Then she shut the door in my face with a loud bang, saying as she did so that she was ashamed to have a spineless brother-in-law like me. My elder sister-in-law is an educated, self-righteous woman. From her perspective, her furious outburst made so much sense.'

'I know,' Hua said deliberately, 'but that may not be fair to you. She was, in fact, too harsh on you, I would say. People cannot help judging from their own perspectives.'

'Like her, there are also a number of Li loyalists being very harsh on me. From their point of view, they're not without their reasons. But I still beg to differ. One has to be loyal, first of all, to the welfare of the Tang people. Not necessarily to one particular person, whether surnamed Li or Wu.'

'That's a valid point, Your Honor. Mencius has said something just like that too.'

'I would also like to add,' Judge Dee said, 'that however notorious and lascivious the empress appears to be in the people's gossip, she's still a capable, competent ruler. She has been doing her best for the Tang Empire in her way. You have to admit that the Tang dynasty has been enjoying prosperity under her rule.

And things are quite peaceful too – except, that is, for the recent rebellion led by General Xu.'

'Again, you have a point. But as we have discussed, other people may also have their points. You must have heard of the scandalous affair between the empress and Monk Xue?'

'Yes, people can argue on and on. But enough of the political debates, Doctor Hua. Let's switch topics. You talked quite a lot with Luo when he stayed with you for treatment in the hut here, I have been told.'

'I'm a huge fan of Luo's poetry. He is one of the most excellent poets of our time. In my opinion, he's definitely number one among the Tang Empire's "four most excellent". As for me, I'm just a poor, unsuccessful candidate in the civil service examination, and I do not have one-tenth of his poetic talent. So it meant a lot for me to have the opportunity of talking and discussing with him.'

'I too wish I could have had such an opportunity, Doctor Hua. I have never met with Luo Binwang in person, but I also like his poetry a lot. Please tell me more about your meeting and talking with him. It's also for my continuous education.'

'In the early stage of the uprising, the rebellious army had won several major battles in quick succession, so they pushed on with unbelievable momentum. A lot of people attributed it to the brilliant and inspiring "Call to Arms" penned by Luo Binwang. But unfortunately, Luo was wounded in one of these battles. General Xu had him moved into this poor hut of mine, so I could take better care of him with my herbal medicine and acupuncture.'

'How serious was his wound?'

'Not that serious. In fact, he remained in high spirits most of the time. He even copied out a poem of his for me about one of the battles fought near the distant borders.'

Hua climbed up into a small attic, and then descended with a silk scroll of the poem titled 'Seeing Off Officer Zheng at the Border'.

Facing the barbarian invasion from the enemy,
our heroic soldiers are marching east,

crossing Shanggan River to defend the country.
The shining arrows keep shooting, tearing
through the dense green willow leaves,
over the white-jade-decorated saddles,
against a blaze of blossoming peach flowers.
The bright moon projects the shadows
of the full-stretched bows to the ground,
with stars gathering around the tip
of the gigantic sword suspended in the sky.

Oh, don't be like a failed assassin
in the ancient times, singing,
in vain, the sad, sentimental song
of 'Chilly Wind by Yi River'.

There was a line underneath the poem in smaller characters: 'Copying an old poem for my good doctor and friend Hua – as a token of my sincere gratitude to him for the miraculous treatment during my convalescence at his home.'

So Luo had not written the poem specifically for Hua, but just copied it out. Judge Dee had no idea who 'Officer Zheng' was in the title of the poem. Still, such a copy in Luo's own calligraphy along with the dedication would mean a lot to a man of letters.

'It's a wonderful poem,' Judge Dee said, nodding. 'The last stanza is full of intertextual allusions to the failed assassin, Jin Ke, at the beginning of the Qing Empire. It could also serve as a sort of self-portrait of Luo Binwang. Not to mention the fact that it's copied in his own calligraphy, with your name mentioned as well. As a highly collectable item, the scroll may be truly invaluable. Make sure you keep it in a safe and proper place, Doctor Hua. It takes a poet of Luo's caliber to produce a masterpiece like this.'

'Who could have thought that, shortly afterward, General Xu's army would suffer such a stunning defeat, from which they would never recover?' Dr Hua said. 'Nobody could have anticipated such an abrupt, irrecoverable turn in the civil war. It's just like in an old saying: the defeated army is fleeing away, as helter-skelter as if they were in the midst of collapsing mountains and crushing earthquakes.'

'You're absolutely right about that, Hua. The situation on the battlefield can change so dramatically overnight. What happened to Luo then?'

'Luo believed that he had pretty much recovered, and he insisted on going back to the front. It would have been safer for him to rest for another week or so. I tried my best to dissuade him, but without success. Perhaps that's just like him – an idealistic "frontier poet", fighting and writing for what he really believes in.'

'Perhaps he realized that his aspirations could also vanish like a curl of smoke with the impeding tragic end of the uprising. But Luo has never contacted you since?'

'No, he has not. It wasn't easy for people to contact one another during the time of the rebellion. Besides, I'm definitely not someone that important to him. And, of course, Luo could have been killed in the last battle.'

Judge Dee thought he could detect a ring of truth in the response made by Hua, who had talked matter-of-factly without any furtive changes in his expression.

It was also true that Luo himself had a lot to worry about as the rebellion army began to suffer one big defeat after another.

'By the way, I've just gathered some rare herbs in the mountains this morning. You look a bit tired. The herbs might serve as a tune-up for your Yin-Yang system, Your Honor. Would you like to try them? All are natural, fresh, organic – a tonic for the system. At the very least, the medicine won't hurt or have any side effects.'

His words were like a subtle signal. *No more on the topic of Luo Binwang, please.*

Judge Dee understood only too well the reasons behind this request. Hua had every reason to be extra-cautious. He had already been repeatedly interrogated by secret agents from the capital and must have shared his information about Luo a thousand times.

But Judge Dee decided not to leave immediately. He might be able to pick up something else in his ongoing conversation with Hua, he thought.

Dr Hua moved over to a small wood-burning stove, put a variety of herbs into an earthen urn and started preparing a herbal drink for Judge Dee.

'Normally, one-third of the herbs would be enough for a couple of doses. So, I'm making six doses for you, Your Honor. Enough for three days. One dose in the morning and another in the evening.'

So Judge Dee and Dr Hua sat around the stove, and Hua delivered a long, serious lecture about the miracle of traditional herbal medicine. It was a speech full of concrete details as well as illustrations from the fresh herbs nearby. Dee listened attentively, making numerous notes and nodding in response.

Judge Dee finally rose and bid farewell to his host. After about three hours spent in Hua's hut, however, Dee did not think he had gained anything substantial or relevant regarding the case of Luo Binwang.

SIX

No man is an island,
Entire of itself.
Each is a piece of the continent,
A part of the main.
If a clod be washed away by the sea,
Europe is the less.
As well as if a promontory were.
As well as if a manor of thy friend's
Or of thine own were:
Each man's death diminishes me,
For I am involved in mankind.
Therefore, send not to know
For whom the bell tolls,
It tolls for thee.

– John Donne

'True wisdom comes to each of us when we realize how little we understand about life, ourselves, and the world around us.'

– Socrates

What with the greenish herbal drink Dr Hua had carefully prepared for him and the joyful chorus of chirping birds outside the hostel window, Judge Dee woke up the next morning feeling rested and refreshed.

He raised the paper window to the courtyard, to see it scattered with fallen petals after a long night's rain and wind. The scene unexpectedly evoked for him the lines written by Men Haoran, another celebrated contemporary poet of the Tang Empire.

How we have overslept this spring morning!
Here, there, everywhere, birds
are heard chirping, twittering.

After a long night's clamor
of wind and rain, how many petals
have fallen down to the ground?

But it was not a spring morning; Judge Dee knew that only too well.

Stepping out of the hostel in the morning light, he yawned, rubbed his eyes and saw Yang had already placed several more soft cushions in the carriage for him.

'There may be a long day of travel ahead of us, and you have long suffered from terrible backache. You cannot take too much care of yourself, Master,' Yang said grumpily and cracked the whip loudly in the air. It was probably meant as a demonstration of his continuous protest against the investigation that had been pushed forcefully on to his weak, elderly master.

'You're being so considerate, Yang.'

'Where is the next stop for us, Master?'

'The Shu River.'

Yang did not ask why. He merely repeated a crack of the whip in front of the carriage.

Judge Dee was ready to set out, climbing slowly into the carriage, when Mayor Zhuang came over with enough snacks and water for a journey of at least two days.

Mayor Zhuang bowed repeatedly to Judge Dee, silhouetted by a tall, sweeping willow tree by the hostel door, even as the carriage moved away.

Soon the road became bumpy again, and Judge Dee felt increasingly grateful for the soft cushions Yang had prepared for him. These long trips were proving to be a bit too much for a man of his age. With the carriage curtains pulled down, however, he found himself feeling fairly comfortable. Warm and drowsy, it was as if he were wrapped in a soft silkworm cocoon.

The talk with Dr Hua had left behind a vague feeling of uneasiness. But Judge Dee could not put his finger on it. He did not think he had to take it too seriously, though.

The unpopularity of the empress among the men of letters was practically tangible. Much more so after the release of that powerful 'Call to Arms' penned by Luo Binwang. As for the sensational, salacious speculation about her private life in the declaration, it was not something new or secret to a lot of common people.

Despite the bumpy carriage, Judge Dee tried to concentrate on any details in his talk with Dr Hua that he might have overlooked, considering things piece by piece, sentence by sentence, until an unexpected wave of sleepiness overtook him . . .

And then he was startled out of his nap by a violent jolt at a sharp turn of the road. Glancing out through a crack in the carriage curtain, Judge Dee was greeted by the sight of a blue jay flashing up high into the azure sky. Puffs of wind kept inclining lanky hollyhocks by the roadside toward the carriage. A yellow dog was loitering in the checked shade in front of a farmhouse.

Judge Dee was relieved to see the carriage was moving close to a quaint village embosomed in verdant trees and bushes, but it was perhaps too early for them to take a break there.

Rubbing his eyes again, he thought he heard the sound of horse hooves beating the ground furiously from not too far a distance, drawing nearer on a spur. When he lifted the carriage curtain high, the judge caught sight of a black-clad man galloping after them in great haste.

Yang too started looking over his shoulder, on high alert, and exclaimed in a subdued voice, 'There's someone on a horse behind us, Master. Hurrying straight toward us!'

It soon became obvious that it was a black-attired messenger who was hurrying down the ancient path after them. Judge Dee ordered Yang to halt the carriage.

When the messenger's horse was abreast with the carriage, he reined in his horse and handed a letter to Judge Dee through the window. He was still panting as he did so, out of breath from riding over at full speed.

'His Excellency, Mayor Zhuang, wanted me to hurry and hand this letter to you before you got too far away.'

They had only parted about an hour or so earlier. Why send a messenger in such a hurry? Snatching the letter out of the envelope, Judge Dee started reading it in the carriage.

'Doctor Hua was found dead in his hut this morning, according to one of his neighbors,' Mayor Zhuang had written. 'To be more exact, he was savagely beheaded with a sharp cleaver. It's said that his body was lying in pools of blood, as if in a slaughterhouse. I'm on my way to his hut right now.

'Why would somebody want to kill a harmless herbal doctor like Hua? Since you interviewed him just the previous day, would you like to come back to look into it, Your Honor?'

Judge Dee was too dumbfounded to give an instant answer. There was an unmistakable unspoken message in Mayor Zhuang's letter. It pointed to a concealed connection between Judge Dee's visit and Dr Hua's murder.

And Judge Dee thought so too. For reasons beyond him, Dr Hua had been murdered just after his face-to-face talk with the judge. The good old doctor did not agree with him on everything, Judge Dee knew, but Hua was a respectable man of integrity.

The secret police had interrogated him more than once and found nothing of interest. But could Dr Hua's murder really have been related to Judge Dee's unannounced visit?

Everything is possible, though not pardonable. However hard he tried, Judge Dee still failed to see any logical connection between his visit and Hua's violent death.

Now what was he going to do?

As Judge Dee could not manage to come up with any plausible theories for why he could have caused Hua's death, the close sequence of events could have been just a coincidence. As an experienced investigating judge, however, Judge Dee did not believe in so-called coincidences.

Nor did he see any point in hurrying back to Dr Hua's hut right at this moment. For one thing, that would not be what the empress would want him to do. Discovering his actions through her omnipresent secret police, she might see it as something like purposeful procrastination on his part. With the gigantic surveillance network of the Tang Empire, she could easily have had him shadowed all the way here. In the final analysis, he had never pledged exclusive loyalty to the Wu family.

Besides, Judge Dee still could not see a plausible motive that connected his investigation into Luo's disappearance to Hua's subsequent murder. So returning to the scene of the crime would not help him with his current case, but just distract him from his duty.

Luo had stayed in Dr Hua's company for a fortnight. Hua had taken care of Luo's wound, and the treatment had made a difference to the latter's quick recovery. It would have been natural for Luo to feel grateful to Dr Hua for his help. But then Luo had had no choice but to set out in a hurry to take part in the last disastrous battle by the Wuding River.

After Lu's return to the battlefield, it was natural, too, that there would have been no possibility for Luo and Hua to meet up again. The secret police had already interrogated Hua and had found nothing; if they had, Judge Dee would not have been sent out on this wild goose chase to track down a rebel poet who was evidently already dead.

Therefore, Judge Dee decided not to go back. He wrote to Mayor Zhuang instead.

'Being entrusted with Her Majesty's mission, I cannot afford to have too long a delay here. I know that you will surely do your best to investigate the Hua murder case and catch the killer. It means a lot to me. I trust your capability.

'Gather all the evidence and the related information regarding this diabolical case, Mayor Zhuang. Don't rule out any possible theories too quickly. Keep me posted all the way. If needs be, use the fastest delivery available to send any new information to me. All the necessary expense will be covered as a part of the top government work under Her Majesty.

'It was a pleasant surprise to meet you, Zhuang,' Judge Dee wrote at the conclusion of the letter. 'You have been following in my footsteps, doing a good job in local government and acting as a real investigating judge too. Someday, when you come to the Chang'an capital for a visit, I'll introduce you to my colleagues as an excellent student of mine.'

As the black-attired messenger left in a swirl of dust, galloping on his way back to Mayor Zhuang, Judge Dee was hit with the realization that he had come out in a cold, clammy sweat. His long gown was drenched – too drenched for him to go back to sleep any time soon.

The road became full of jolts and jerks again. He heard the lonely cry of a wild goose through the distant sky, and then saw the bird losing itself in a bank of gray clouds.

'Alas, I did not kill Hua, but he died because of me,' Judge Dee murmured to himself again, almost inaudibly, parodying the same ancient Chinese saying.

On horseback in front of the carriage, Yang appeared still to be shaking his head in resignation. As Judge Dee's assistant, working alongside him for so long, he must have known that it would be useless to try to dissuade him from going on with the dangerous mission. He must know, too, that right now, instead of taking a much-needed nap against the soft cushions in the carriage, his master was conjuring up various theories to explain the vicious murder.

After a couple of hours on the road, Judge Dee told Yang to take a lunch break by the roadside.

'You have been driving the carriage along this difficult road since the morning. No need to speed on like this, Yang.'

'I'm fine, Master,' Yang protested, but Dee insisted.

They seated themselves under an ash tree, munching green onion cakes and drinking from a bamboo container of freshly squeezed watermelon juice.

'What do you think, Master?'

'About what?'

'About the murder of Hua, of course, just one day after your unannounced visit to his hut.'

'It's too much of a coincidence; you're right about that. I cannot put my finger on there being a definite connection between the two,' Judge Dee said. 'On the other hand, I don't think I can rule out the possibility just yet.'

'So what are you going to do?'

'I've written a letter to the mayor. Hopefully, he will do his level best to solve the herbal doctor's vicious murder. I bet he will. Mayor Zhuang is a clever, capable man. Alas, though. I'm really responsible for Hua's death.'

'You mustn't say that. We don't know anything for sure – not yet. But what are we going do when we reach the Shu River?'

'We are going to find a fishing girl nicknamed Little Swallow.'

'Little Swallow?'

'What happened between Luo and Little Swallow in a sampan on the Shu River could be considered a complicated story. I'll tell you more about it this evening.'

Shortly after their lunch, they resumed their journey, and a blue-headed fly stumbled into the soft-cushioned carriage, buzzing, flipping, humming and circling the fatigued Judge Dee.

The inside of the carriage grew more and more suffocating. It was cold outside, he knew. He pulled up the curtain and waved his hand about forcefully. The droning ceased. The moment the curtain fell back down, however, the monotonous noise returned, more insistent than before.

He felt unbearably bugged.

He was, after all, in his sixties. Traveling so long on the uneven road, working on theories concerning the murder of the late herbal doctor Hua, enduring the company of the insistent fly, it all added to a feeling of bone-deep weariness . . .

One or two hours later, Judge Dee woke up with a start from another horrible dream. His sweat-soaked robe clung tight, clammy and uncomfortable against his body. An unexpected sense of impotent déjà vu gripped him.

In the dream, a monstrous black dragon with a white fox's tail was glaring down from a high palace beam, a drop of steaming saliva hitting Judge Dee's sweaty forehead. He turned and looked at his own reflection, shivering with distortion, in a rusted bronze mirror, the candle beside it burning down to ashes. He seemed to hear the night watchman beating his bamboo knocker frantically around the city wall, shouting, 'Fire, fire, fire—'

Judge Dee jumped up in panic, still lost in reeling disorientation. As if in mysterious correspondence, a flower vase fell off its mahogany stand, crashing to the floor with a loud bang—

His devoted assistant Yang curbed the carriage to a hasty stop and asked tremulously over his shoulder, 'Everything is OK with you, my master?'

'Oh, yes, everything is fine. Just another scary dream. Nothing to worry about, Yang.'

'So many bad dreams on this long journey. Let's take a break. She should not have sent you out, traveling so far, far away from the capital, in the first place.'

'I cannot say no to her; you know why. Several times, the empress has declared me to be a pillar of the empire at the court, and to be fair to her, she has treated me as such. I could not but have appreciated it. Just as in an old saying, if someone takes you seriously as a pillar of the state, you have no option but to continue to stand staunch and upright.'

'But the rebellion has been crushed! Luo's nobody but a feeble scribe now, without the strength to kill a goose. What big trouble would he be able to stir up? She could have sent someone else – someone younger and stronger – to carry out this investigation.'

'I don't know about that. The empress is taking the case so seriously. How could I have kept saying no to her? In fact, I've made several unpleasant suggestions to her in my time, but she has never rebuffed me too harshly. She has made a point of showing me the highest respect in the royal court.

'As I've told you before, there was one time when she had just taken a bath, but she still ran out barefoot to usher me in for a long discussion. And she said she was simply imitating the high honor the first Han dynasty emperor had paid to a wise minister. Confucius says, a man will be ready to lay down his life for the one who appreciates him, and a woman will be willing to make herself beautiful for the one who appreciates her—'

'You have told me this anecdote several times already, my Master. You're too much of a Confucian scholar sometimes.'

'You are probably right, I think. I may be just "a totally useless scholar writing" as depicted in a poem written by Luo Binwang – or by another poet in his association. Alas, my poor memory is failing me again.'

SEVEN

'Truth Lord, but I have marred them: let my shame
Go where it doth deserve.
And know you not, says Love, who bore the blame?
My dear, then I will serve.
You must sit down, says Love, and taste my meat:
So I did sit and eat.'

– George Herbert

'There are no facts, only interpretations.'

– Friedrich Nietzsche

'Be kind, for everyone you meet is fighting a hard battle.'

– Plato

In a hurry, in a great hurry,
mountains and passes are left
behind, like in fading dreams . . .

Waking up on the morning when they finally reached the Shu River, Judge Dee murmured these lines to himself. He could not help wondering whether they had somehow come out of his fading dream.

Looking out of the carriage window, he saw a curl of blue smoke rising from a huddle of roofs. Could it be just another scene in the dream? The sight served as another depressing reminder of Hua's hut, with its weather-worn thatched roof trembling in the wind.

Was Hua's cold, stiff body still lying there, in the midst of those pools of blood? Judge Dee again was thunderstruck by the thought.

Along the river's banks, new willow shoots appeared, glistening with the morning rain. Under one tall willow tree, he caught sight of several young men of letters gathering under a white tent. They were holding a farewell party, singing the celebrated parting poem composed by the well-known contemporary poet Wang Wei.

The dust of the Wei City
Moistened by the morning rain,
the willow shoots so young,
so green by the hostel—'Drink,
drink one more cup, my dear friend!
Once out of the Yang Pass,
heading to the west, you'll find
no companion from the old days.

Judge Dee chose to check into a willow-shaded riverside hostel nearby. He thought he needed a much-deserved break.

Following Judge Dee's instructions, Yang tethered the carriage horse at a sturdy tree near the hostel's gate and then walked out to collect more information about the fishing girl nicknamed Little Swallow. He was also going to book the special boat meal with Little Swallow on behalf of his master for the night.

It turned out to be another job drastically different from Yang's imagination. Little Swallow's special sampan meals appeared to be extremely popular. She was already fully booked for the next few months.

Yang eventually managed to approach Little Swallow in person. A young, swarthy and athletic girl, she didn't seem to be very interested in a new customer. Yang talked to her on a pier for a couple of minutes, offering a higher price, much higher than the one that had already been paid for tonight's meal. But she would not budge, refusing to make a change to the pattern of her normal business practice.

Yang knew that Judge Dee could not afford to wait here for months just to try Little Swallow's special sampan meal.

And Judge Dee also knew, only too well, that he could not afford to wait for such a long time. So when Yang told him the bad news, he knew he had no option but to seek help from a local official. He decided to make an unannounced visit to the mayor, surnamed Qian.

'I did not want to bother you, Mayor Qian, but I have a direct order from Her Majesty to carry out an investigation into the disappearance of Luo Binwang. Her Majesty expects a quick conclusion – as quick as possible.'

Mayor Qian did not claim himself as a student of Judge Dee's, but he knew better than to not offer help. To the mayor, Judge Dee was not just a judge, but a mighty, high-ranking minister closely connected to the empress. After all, how could an ordinary judge have been entrusted with such a sensitive investigation unless he had a powerful background? Judge Dee was known for his deep involvement in current Tang politics, which was full of dark, dangerous conspiracies.

'It's a great honor for me to be able to do something for Your Honor. You are entrusted with this highly sensitive investigation by Her Majesty,' Mayor Qian said deliberately. 'As far as the fishing girl is concerned, I don't think it will be too much of a problem for me to arrange something with Little Swallow today. If need be, I can cancel her business license with immediate effect. She is well known, with a large number of followers. But her business is in a sort of gray area, as Your Honor may know.'

'Thank you so much, Mayor Qian. That's a great help. If possible, please arrange the meeting to be a private one. I'd really appreciate it. It goes without saying that no one else needs to know anything about tonight's special sampan meal.'

About an hour later, Judge Dee was told that the mayor had succeeded in booking Little Swallow for dinner that evening – including the night too, if necessary. All the expenses had been paid in advance. It's just as a popular saying goes: In the world of red dust, it takes a powerful official to get things done.

And late that afternoon, stepping down the pier toward Little Swallow's sampan, moored by the riverbank, Judge Dee did not know how the meeting would work out, or how long it would take. A lot of people were milling around the pier, talking, laughing, bargaining, jostling, elbowing each other aside, almost like in a noisy market.

Seeing Little Swallow's sampan was fairly small, Judge Dee asked Yang to wait on the crowded pier. When the sampan started paddling out into the river, Yang might be able to keep it in sight. It should not move out too far.

Soon enough, Little Swallow exited the boat and almost glided toward him. Barefoot, and wearing a homespun red *dudou*-like corset top, it seemed as if she was stepping out of a traditional Chinese painting.

Little Swallow was a fine-featured girl, vivacious, radiant with a healthy tan. Considering how often she had to dive deep into the water for the catch of the day, Judge Dee did not wonder about her scant clothing – or her popularity. She would have appeared irresistibly enticing to a bookish yet romantic man like Luo, he thought. And, for that matter, to a lot of other customers too.

She led him carefully on to the sampan. The boat's shelter, with its bamboo hard top, was tiny, presumably to make more room for the kitchen area on the deck. Once Judge Dee was onboard, amidst the pots and pans, there was not much space left for her, but she still moved around agilely, a pair of anklets gleaming, tinkling over her bare ankles.

A short poem written by Li Bai flashed into Judge Dee's mind.

A fine-featured pretty girl, fair
like a bright moon in the night sky,
wearing no socks, her bare feet
white like frost in wooden sandals.

In the Tang time, under the Confucianist orthodoxy, the convention was for marriages to be arranged. Young girls were not supposed to mix with young men before marriage, let alone date of their own free will. And the list of taboos that were against convention went on and on – young women were not allowed to walk out barefoot, not allowed to wear anything sensual in public, not even allowed to touch hands with the opposite sex . . .

Because of that, Little Swallow oozed an exotic attraction to her customers, like a beam of dancing fire, attracting the fatally doomed moths.

To Judge Dee's surprise, Little Swallow didn't seem to be that interested in talking with him. At best, her manner could be described as business-like, even though she said she'd heard he was an honest, capable, high-ranking official at court and was highly trusted by Her Majesty. Consequently, she said, the local mayor had insisted she go all out to entertain such a 'distinguished guest' as him.

'The weather is so fine today. Perfect for a special meal on deck, Your Honor,' she said, tossing her long black hair in the breeze. In the background, two or three white water birds were fluttering up and down in the air.

The sampan started paddling slowly into the river, amid the splashing waves and ripples. A dragonfly came gliding over, circling in curiosity, before it perched on the unused oar leaning aside.

Still talking glibly, she started bustling around a small earthen stove she had moved up on the deck: lighting the fire with dry twigs, blowing on to it with her shapely mouth, sharpening a knife on a stone, ladling fresh water into several urns and spreading colorful ingredients on a wooden board to the side of the stove . . .

Judge Dee had gathered more information, from here and there, about Luo and Little Swallow, although the reports were not that reliable. He'd heard she was someone capable of singing folk songs, and that she was particularly known for a series called 'Bamboo Twig Songs'. This was a group of beautiful, rhythmic folk songs, which had been edited and revised by a brilliant Tang dynasty poet named Liu Yuxi, and Judge Dee thought they could definitely count as poetry. So, as a talented singer of these songs, Little Swallow might have had some common language – if not a lot – with Luo.

While Little Swallow busied herself with the dinner preparations, Judge Dee talked to her as if he were a conventional customer, full of curious questions. He asked her about tonight's special sampan menu, about her business in general and about this and that, before he brought up Luo's name in a seemingly casual way.

'Quite a number of celebrities have come to your boat, I hear, including Luo Binwang,' he said. 'I think I'm really lucky today.'

'Luo Binwang? I don't recall the name.'

Little Swallow's response dismayed him. Particularly because the nonchalant manner in which she said it convinced Judge Dee that her answer was truthful.

'No, I cannot recall him, not at all,' she repeated categorically, shaking her head like a pretty rattle drum.

Then, with most of the dinner preparation done, she moved toward the bow of the sampan, where she stood and started warbling a song in a sweet voice.

Red peach blossoms blaze
all over the mountains
with the green spring waters
of the Shu River circling.

The flowers will easily fade,
my lord, like your passion,
while the water flows on,
never-ending, like my feelings.

She had an enchanting voice, but the way she was singing – slightly mechanical, or perhaps artificial – struck Judge Dee as being just part of her business practice, like that of diving into the river with a splash, of catching live fish in her bare hands and of cooking there and then on the deck of the boat.

It seemed to be all done for the sake of business. Little wonder she could not remember a particular customer's name – even that of someone like Luo Binwang. The romantic stories about Luo and Little Swallow, told by men of letters, were proving to be nothing but hearsay and fantasy. Luo had had a poor, tough life, and some fans of his poetry, sympathetic to his miseries, could have chosen to make up those amorous tales and add a touch of bright color to his otherwise somber existence.

It spelled that Judge Dee would most likely get nowhere if he continued investigating in this direction. In the end, the research he'd done into Luo and Little Swallow's relationship, as luck would have it, appeared to have been a total waste of effort.

A white fish was jumping in the river, splashing up myriads

of beads of water. Judge Dee looked down, gazing at the white jasmine bud in his teacup, and then over at the bare back of the young fishing girl kneeling in front of him, bending over the ingredients she'd prepared so far for the sampan dinner. He was surprised at the sight of something like a fly stuck on the bare sole of one of her feet – or was it merely a smudge, picked up from the deck? Judge Dee knew he was getting old, his vision failing more and more.

This could turn out to be his last case . . .

'I'm a sentimental old fool,' he murmured to himself, almost inaudibly, with a touch of self-satire, in an attempt to ridicule himself out of his strange mood, 'wandering around, spellbound in the midst of the blossoming flowers.'

He should leave her boat. Today was not a day for him to indulge himself with an exotic sampan meal, however delicious it might taste. He had to cut his losses and—

But he was jerked out of his thoughts by the sight of Little Swallow jumping into the river. She dived in with a graceful curve, swam like a mermaid, striking out her arms rhythmically, splashing up infinite diamonds into the late-afternoon light.

So, she was diving into the water to make the well-known 'live catch of the day'.

The local mayor would have put a lot of pressure on her. Judge Dee knew that Little Swallow had no choice but to perform her best for a distinguished guest like him. And he knew better than to imagine she could have any romantic interest in a fat, old man like him.

The surface of the river was growing calm again, and hardly any ripples were visible in the gradually fading light. Little Swallow had vanished out of sight, but Judge Dee wasn't too worried. She was known for her extraordinary diving skills.

And in any case, his mind was wandering back to the Luo case, helplessly, as if he were obsessed.

Dusk is approaching fast,
where is my faraway home?
The scene of mist-and-smoke-covered river
only adds to the melancholy . . .

Judge Dee heaved a long sigh and stood up. He was moving to the sampan's stern, the wind fitful, when she shot out of the water like a flying fish. She was carrying live bass and mandarin fish, and crabs were struggling in a string net attached to her slender waist. The silver bangles around her ankles glittered and jingled as she swam back toward the solitary sampan.

She was peddling the water effortlessly. The soles of her bare feet shone pinkish in the shifting light reflecting from the sampan – then inexplicably juxtaposed with the red webbed feet of a snow-white goose, which also seemed to come out of nowhere, like a mysterious apparition in the ripples of the river.

Little Swallow started murmuring, 'Goo, goo, goo . . .' as she swam near, while the mystical goose circled the sampan's bow.

In a trance, Judge Dee felt as if he himself had metamorphosed into a goose, all of a sudden, under the young girl's gaze. He could not help it – the first few lines of the well-known poem penned by Luo burst out of him.

'Goo, goo, goo!'
Arching its neck,
the goose is singing
to the high skies . . .

Little Swallow climbed back into the sampan, her wet feet leaving a line of footprints on the deck, her eyes mirroring the surprise on Judge Dee's face.

'Were you reciting a poem, Little Swallow?' Judge Dee said, eying the young girl up and down. 'The poem titled "Ode to a Goose".'

'Oh, you know it too, Your Honor? Yes, I was.'

'Have you read a lot of poems?'

'No, hardly any. But in my childhood, I often heard other kids singing that poem in their gardens. My parents were too poor to send me to school, but those days when I could listen to a poem like that, and learn to sing it, those were happy ones. Alas, my parents passed away when I was barely a teenager.'

'I am so sorry to hear that, Little Swallow.'

'After the death of my parents, I had to support myself in one way or another, you know? I've grown up by the river, and I turned into a so-called fishing girl—'

'What's wrong with that, Little Swallow? You should be proud of yourself. You are capable of supporting yourself with your hard work and extraordinary skill.'

Standing up on the deck, Judge Dee started to recite the poem 'Ode to a Goose' from beginning to end:

> *'"Goo, goo, goo!"*
> *Arching its neck,*
> *the goose is singing*
> *to the high skies,*
> *white feathers drifting*
> *over the green water,*
> *and red webs pedaling*
> *in the clear ripples.'*

'Yes, that's it. That's the very poem sung by other girls in the garden, Your Honor!'

'Is there anyone living under the sun of the great Tang Empire who does not know this poem? "Ode to a Goose" presents an innocent and beautiful picture of the children and the goose amusing themselves, blending into each other. It is written from a child's perspective, observing the goose from the shore, and it is easy to picture the scene. The goose, singing in the water, seems to be teasing the children. The children, craning their necks at the scene, imitate the "goo, goo, goo" sound. We can easily imagine that, in reaction to the children's teasing, the big white goose swims more vigorously and sings more cheerfully.'

'You're so right about that, Your Honor. I did not know it's such a famous poem.'

'This poem is so simple, so natural. At first, young children, who have not learned to speak, can only utter the sound of "goo, goo, goo" . . . until the word "goose" finally bursts blissfully out of their mouths. When read aloud by children, their joy and the joy of the white goose smoothly converge into one. However, the poem is not just for children. It works for adult readers too, because it successfully evokes a provocative vision of lost innocence at the depth of their hearts.'

'Wow, your interpretation makes the poem even more beautiful to me, and more meaningful. You are a profound scholar. I really appreciate your help, Your Honor.'

'"Ode to a Goose" is extremely popular among the literati, as well as the ordinary people. But can you guess who wrote this fantastic poem, Little Swallow?'

'Who?'

'Luo Binwang. The poet I've just asked you about.'

'The poet you have just asked me about? Oh, no. That's not possible – it was not written by a man of that name.'

'And from what I have learned,' Judge Dee pressed, 'that renowned poet once stayed with you on this sampan for a couple of nights.'

'A renowned poet stayed with me for a couple of nights on the boat?' she murmured, as if questioning herself, incredulity written clearly on her face.

Leaving the question unanswered, she tied her hair up with a long wooden pin, threw two or three crabs into a steaming pot and turned to scale the small-mouth bass, which was still jumping vigorously on the bamboo cutting board.

Why Luo Binwang had chosen to stay for a couple of nights on her boat, Judge Dee thought he could understand.

'I once had a customer who did not give me his name,' she said, looking up. 'He simply called himself a pathetic, down-and-out bookworm. He came to me merely as a customer, like others, not as an important man.'

'I think I know why.'

'But I did not know—' She took a short pause before going on. 'Anyway, he *did* look like a down-and-out bookworm to me. He told me he was the author of the goose poem and recited it for me from beginning to end. I thought the poem was just doggerel for children, not a famous work by a renowned poet.

'But, because of my precious childhood memory, you know, I felt obliged to do something for him – something small, in my own way. My customers usually pay me a fairly high price for a special boat meal, but he was apparently not that well-off. It happened to be the low fishing season, so I invited him to stay for free on the boat for a couple of days . . .'

'It's like an archetype from classical Chinese literature. A young beauty falls in love with a man who's neither wealthy nor famous. She simply adores him for his talent from the bottom of her heart—'

'I don't know what you are talking about, Your Honor. You must be teasing me.'

'No, I'll find a copy of *Story of Liwa* for you, Little Swallow. You should read it, and then you'll understand this archetype from classical Chinese literature . . .'

The sampan was drifting into the middle of the river, purposelessly.

Little Swallow started cooking on the small stove, her clothing still wet, and her face flushing with the fire. She proved to be a well-seasoned chef, moving around light-footedly, throwing in a pinch of brownish salt, and adding a bunch of chopped scallions . . .

Soon a variety of delicacies appeared on a small rough, unpainted wooden table set between the two of them. Slices of sticky-rice-filled lotus root immersed in honey, steamed bass with slices of green onion and golden ginger on top, and a large bowl of minced fish congee strewn with chopped parsley . . . Judge Dee considered that Little Swallow was doing a miraculous job this evening.

The remaining straw-tied crabs made a faint bubbling sound in a sesame-floored pail, while a large mandarin fish thrashed around in another pail, splashing in a desperate struggle. Those were to be cooked later, Judge Dee supposed.

He was raising his chopsticks, ready to taste the steamed bass, when she spun around to stop him, saying, 'Please wait just a minute, Your Honor.'

She bent down to put more slices of green onion and golden ginger, plus several pieces of dried red pepper, on top of the fish, then poured a ladle of sizzling oil over it all. Judge Dee tasted the fish, still sizzling in the white and blue bowl, his mouth watering with a surge of delicious flavor. It was both unbelievably tasty and tender.

'It's worth every penny, I have to say,' Judge Dee said, a large piece of the fish swimming on his tongue, though he had no idea how much the local mayor had paid her. 'You are a super chef, Little Swallow!'

She deftly ladled out a smaller bowl of the steaming hot fish congee, threw in a pinch of white pepper and placed it softly in front of Judge Dee.

A favor from such a beauty as Little Swallow is difficult to pay back. So Luo Binwang must have thought when he was in the company of Little Swallow, Judge Dee concluded, putting a spoonful of the congee into his mouth.

How might Luo Binwang have tried to repay her for her generous hospitality?

In the great Tang Empire, Judge Dee knew that well-known poets enjoyed a high social status, and it was a matter of course for young girls to fall head over heels for them. The civil service examination included poetry as an integral part of it, so an excellent poem could make a huge difference to the final mark.

But this was probably not the case for Little Swallow. She could not read. Luo had not given her his name, and even if he had, she did not know that he was such a popular poet. It was understandable, though, for her to feel warmth towards someone who, out of the blue, claimed to be the author of her beloved goose poem, and, in turn, her innocent reaction to his poem could have rendered her even more attractive in his mind.

'Make another guess. Do you know why I came to find you here, Little Swallow?'

'No, I have no idea at all.'

'It's because of a romantic poem Luo wrote for you.'

Judge Dee then produced a piece of paper out of his long gown. The poem copied on it was the one that Jiong had ferreted out for him at the start of his investigation, when he was still in the capital. 'It is called "Remembering a Beautiful Girl in Shu",' he said, and he read the poem out loud.

East and West, Wu and Shu, so far away
with passes and mountains standing
in the way. Alas, it is too far
for the letter-carrying fish to reach you,
or for the message-bearing wild goose.

Little wonder about the long streaks
of tears on your face, as you recall
the moment that the passionate clouds
turned into hot rain, circling,
caressing in the deep mountains.

Obviously, she did not understand much of the poem. Her face registered only puzzlement.

'Is this poem written for me? Fish . . . but how could a fish have carried a letter for me? And for that matter, why the message-bearing wild goose?'

'Those are frequently used allusions in classic Chinese poetry,' Judge Dee explained. 'For those people far, far away from their dear ones, it was not easy for them to send letters or messages when mountains and rivers were standing in the way. In ancient myths, consequently, a fish or a wild goose came to serve for the imagined postal purpose.'

'But why does the ending of the poem talk about the clouds and rain in the deep mountains?' she asked.

'Well, the most famous sexual love scene in classic poetry takes place in a rhapsody composed by Song Yu in the Spring and Autumn period. It is a fantastic piece about the romantic rendezvous between King Xiang of the Chu State and the Wu Mountain Goddess. The climax of their encounter is described as a white cloud – soft, insubstantial – then as a hot rain – passionate, piercing, pounding . . . So here the poet, Luo Binwang, uses this classic allusion to sexual love in his evocation of the clouds in the mountains toward the end of the poem.'

'But we did not . . .'

She did not have to explain further. Though uneducated, Little Swallow was not stupid. And it was possibly true that nothing like that had happened between the two of them. As an impoverished poet, Luo could not have been the one for her, in any case. Their relationship had lasted for just a couple of nights on the boat, presumably.

Little Swallow was a realistic girl, fighting her own hard battles for survival. On the other hand, as a fishing girl working in a potentially disreputable business, she could only be a hindrance to Luo in his own battle to reach the top. That's probably why Luo had not even told her his real name.

But, as if it were an afterthought, Little Swallow turned around and headed to the tiny cabin. After two or three minutes, she returned to him on the deck, holding something in her hand.

'That down-and-out bookworm left me something, which I saved in my cabin. I can't read, I'm ashamed to admit, so I still have no clue what it is,' Little Swallow said, producing a piece of parchment and handing it to Judge Dee.

After just a glance, Judge Dee saw that it appeared to be another poem composed by Luo Binwang. It did not read, however, like one, as it was not in Luo's usual style. It was actually more like free verse or rhapsody, stylistically reminiscent of the 'Romantic Rendezvous in the Wu Mountains' or 'Ode to Luo Goddess'.

Still, it was provocative in its subject matter, and surrealistic too. Judge Dee could not help wondering – emitting a low whistle as he read on – whether some of the graphic details could indeed have been the product of a despondent poet giving free rein to his wild, drunken imagination, while in the company of a young pretty fishing girl on a drifting sampan. The poem read:

To a Fishing Girl

A drunk traveler, lone, wet, cold,
boarded a sampan on a stormy night,
hungry like a wolf, where a young, pretty
fishing girl welcomed him, kneeling,
wearing a wet dudou-*like corset*
hugging the rise of her breasts,
her feet bare, silver bangles jingling,
lighting up the bamboo boat wall

behind her. She was making a vivid introduction
to the celebrated chef's special
of her sampan, waving the menu
in her hand, explaining the secret recipe
for frying a live mandarin fish.
A large one, with its head and tail sticking
out of the sizzling oil, was frying
in the wok, still turning, trembling.

A small smudge stuck on the arch
of her bare, shapely foot struck his imagination
and he experienced the hallucination
of her turning into a struggling fish
being scooped out of the net.
'Fry just for one minute,
better with an ice cube in its mouth.'

Served under the bamboo awning
of the boat, it tastes so tender, juicy,
melting on the tongue, its eyes goggling
once or twice – or was that something
he imagined in his intoxication?

The fish is turning back into the girl,
bleeding, struggling and thrashing, he
fell to suckling hard at her delicious, delicate toe
like a dainty ball of the fish-cheek meat.

It was a poem imbued with complex, passionate intensity. Judge Dee read it again, even more closely, under the light of a new candle Little Swallow placed on the table, tapping his fingers on its edge.

More likely than not, it could have been a wild sexual fantasy on Luo's part, imagined as Little Swallow prepared the meal on the deck in front of him. A number of details did appear to be real, like her bangles twinkling, jingling over her bare ankles, or like the mandarin fish in her secret recipe, with its still-goggling eyes.

Judge Dee stole another glance at the mandarin fish, thrashing about in the pail full of water. *Could* the poem contain the secret recipe for Little Swallow's eyes-still-googling delicacy? It was a poem that Luo might never have shown to other people. Paradoxically, Little Swallow did not count, since she could not read.

From the perspective of a poetry collector – a role Judge Dee had once so passionately played in the murder case concerning the celebrated poetess Xuanji – the present poem could be very valuable, particularly as it was written in Luo's own calligraphy, on expensive parchment, and it contained a plausible recipe too—

Out of the growing darkness, however, a flash suddenly swished through the air, sweeping over in a glaring curve. Possibly it was another jumping fish, he thought—

But no! It was—

Next to him in the quivering sampan, Little Swallow was swaying, stumbling and finally falling with a thump on the deck, knocking over a pail, the platter in her hand breaking into thousands of pieces, before Judge Dee could have said or done anything to help her.

There was a knife trembling in her throat, and a thin red line immediately started spreading around her body. Little Swallow was lying in a grotesque position at his feet, blood oozing down her barely covered breasts. Her corset string, Judge Dee realized, had been severed by the sharp flying knife.

Gingerly, he bent over her body and reached out to feel her wrist, which was already getting cold, though still wet. He failed to feel a pulse. It was beyond his power to do anything for her, he thought, the realization stabbing him hard.

A breeze rustled through the weeping willows that lined the bank, like a sad, soft elegy. The white goose reemerged out of nowhere, like an apparition, pedaling over as if eager to join in the mourning on the river. Judge Dee was still wondering at the goose's mysterious return, wiping his eyes with the back of his hand, when it began swimming once again out of sight into the dark—

Another flash of light cut through the approaching eventide

toward them. Judge Dee jerked and jumped up in panic, not at all like his usual self; undisturbed composure was more characteristic of the celebrated Judge Dee.

It was indeed another flying knife, attached with hooks and a long rope, aiming at the parchment with Luo's fish fantasy poem written on it. The knife stabbed the parchment with amazing accuracy and was then violently pulled back, carrying the parchment along with it.

The realization sent another chill down Judge Dee's spine. The flying knife must have been thrown from another sampan, one with a black-colored hardtop, which had been floating, Judge Dee recalled, almost in parallel with Little Swallow's. As far as he remembered, there were no other boats sailing on the river at the time. That boat with the black hardtop was, however, spinning around at this moment, and speeding off into the darkness like a specter.

Almost at the same instant, there was another splash in the water, and Judge Dee saw Yang jump headlong into the river from the pier, striking out his arms forcefully, swimming vigorously toward the drifting sampan containing Judge Dee and Little Swallow.

It would prove to be too late, Judge Dee knew, his mouth full of bitterness.

In the ensuing silence, a paragraph he had once read in the *Diamond Sutra* flashed through his mind. At the conclusion of another investigation he'd made, into the murder of a young, beautiful poetess, he recalled that he'd felt inconsolable about her tragic fate, and the celebrated monk poet Han Shan had given Dee a copy of the Sutra to comfort him in his grief.

According to the Buddhist classic, everything is nothing but appearance. If a man clings to the appearance of things, he will never be able to see through the vanities of the world of red dust.

The language of the Sutra had exercised an inexplicable calming effect on Judge Dee. Murmuring the text on the sampan now, he burst into incontrollable sobs, feeling helpless, yet still unable to see through the appearance of the situation to the truth of things like Han Shan would.

'All the appearances of causalities in this world, therefore,

are to be seen like a dream, an illusion, a bubble, a shadow, a drop of dew, or a flash of lightning.'

It was conventional for Buddhist monks to keep on chanting Buddhist scripture for the deceased, pressing the palms, counting beads and kowtowing to the ground, but it would be much too dramatic for Judge Dee to do anything along those lines at the present moment.

Under the black shroud of the night, he could hear the bubbling froth created by the surviving crabs, moistening them as they squeezed against each other in the sesame-covered pail. And then the mandarin fish slipped out of the overturned pail beside Little Swallow's feet, jumping back into the Shu River in the dark.

It might be just as well.

EIGHT

'You have your way. I have my way. As for the right way, the correct way, and the only way, it does not exist.'

– Friedrich Nietzsche

'Ah, love, let us be true
To one another! for the world, which seems
To lie before us like a land of dreams,
So various, so beautiful, so new,
Hath really neither joy, nor love, nor light,
Nor certitude, nor peace, nor help for pain;
And we are here as on a darkling plain
Swept with confused alarms of struggle and flight,
Where ignorant armies clash by night.'

– Matthew Arnold

'Act in such a way that you treat humanity, whether in your own person or in the person of any other, never merely as a means to an end, but always at the same time as an end.'

– Immanuel Kant

Judge Dee woke up with another violent start, his palms sweaty and clammy from his unsuccessful effort to chase off an insistent black bat that had been fizzing in and out of his bad dream.

He shook his head, trying to prevent himself from being engulfed in the most miserable angst. It was still the first gray of the morning. Once again, he felt lost in the midst of the juxtaposition of unbelievable appearance and equally unbelievable reality.

Not too long ago, Judge Dee had murmured to himself, 'I did not kill Hua, but Hua died because of me.' When he'd said it, it had just been a plausible scenario in his mind, not fact.

Now, as he said repeatedly to himself, 'I did not kill Little Swallow, but she died because of me,' he knew, without any doubt in his mind, that it was true.

She had died as collateral damage, at the very least, of the investigation, her death ordered and orchestrated by the empress from her throne in the capital of Chang'an. Perhaps he could choose to say neither death had anything to do with him, to make himself feel a little better, but there was no denying the role he'd played, unwittingly or not, in bringing about both fatal tragedies.

He had interviewed Dr Hua and Little Swallow in the course of his investigation – and both had died. And that was to say nothing of Ning, the former Empress Wang's maid, whose suspicious death had occurred before he'd even left the capital.

Judge Dee was suddenly angry. While he was not certain whether the death of Ning was connected to his investigation, he was pretty sure about the causality of Dr Hua's death, and he had now witnessed Little Swallow's death with his own eyes, and felt her young, vibrant body getting cold, rigid, her life flowing away in his arms. But far more than that, Little Swallow was not involved in the gruesome politics at the top – not at all – and yet she'd still died in his company.

So the investigation now became something personal to Judge Dee. He had to do something for Little Swallow. Although she had perished, he still had to push the investigation to the bitter end.

After breakfast in the hostel canteen, Yang placed a shallow fire basin in front of the hostel. He lit the fire and insisted on Judge Dee stepping over it no fewer than three times. That was another popular superstitious practice. It supposedly helped to fight off bad luck and any evil spirits that had gathered after a recent death. It was turning out to be an ill-starred investigation indeed, with three innocent people already having bitten the red dust in the course of it.

Before the fire had even burned out in the basin, Mayor Qian arrived at the hostel, hurrying over in an unpainted bamboo sedan chair and stepping over the fire basin after Judge Dee.

'I'm so sorry for what happened on the boat yesterday, Your Honor,' Mayor Qian said miserably. 'It must have been a devastating shock to you, I know, and I take full responsibility for it. This is my jurisdiction. And I give you my word: a thorough investigation into the fishing girl's death is the order of the day for me today.'

'I'm fine, Mayor Qian,' Judge Dee said, having decided not to go into details about his suspicions over who committed the murder in the sampan. 'It might have been an assassination attempt aimed at me; unfortunately, it killed Little Swallow instead. But for the important assignment from Her Majesty, I should have stayed here to further investigate Little Swallow's death alongside you. I am so sorry and feel so responsible for it.

'So leave no stone unturned in your investigation into her death. She died beside me, her body gradually getting cold on the deck of the drifting sampan. Alas, I did not kill Little Swallow, but she died because of me.'

Judge Dee debated whether he should ask Mayor Qian some straightforward questions. He then thought better of it. The judge was not too sure about the mayor. In the empire's powerful net of surveillance, whatever he chose to say could be reported to the empress. At this critical juncture, Judge Dee felt he had better not ask too many questions about those deaths.

'It's so noble of you to say that, but you really don't have to feel like that about her death,' Mayor Qian replied. 'I will definitely exert my utmost, Your Honor.'

It never rains but it pours.

The unpainted sedan chair containing Mayor Qian had barely moved out of sight when Judge Dee heard a clatter of horse hooves galloping over toward the hostel in haste.

The panting rider handed Judge Dee a letter from Mayor Zhuang near the Wuding River area. An investigation report regarding the murder of Dr Hua. According to the letter, the scenario that his murder had been caused by neighborhood squabble had been ruled out by the mayor, as an eyewitness claimed that he saw a couple of mysterious black-attired men sneaking into the backyard of Hua's hut not long before the horrible tragedy.

Judge Dee was furious.

'Where are we going today, Master?' Yang said, the moment Judge Dee finished reading the letter from Mayor Zhuang, his hands still shaking a little.

'To the Dingguo Temple.'

'The Dingguo Temple? Is that the one in that mountainous province?'

'Yes, that's it. Do you know the way?'

'It's quite a long trip from here. More than a day's travel, I'm afraid. I happen to know its location because one of my uncles used to live in the temple's neighborhood.'

'That's good. You may pay a visit to your uncle. For a change, we may choose to stay in that well-known temple for a couple of days when we arrive. This must have been an exhausting journey for you too, Yang.'

'What do you have up—' Yang did not finish the question with the phrase 'your sleeve'. Judge Dee had long, long sleeves, so to speak. Yang had encountered quite many sudden, surprising changes of plans on Judge Dee's part.

'Whatever you decide to do, you don't have to stay at the temple itself, Master,' Yang continued. 'It won't be difficult to find a decent hostel or a cozy inn nearby, where you can relax far more comfortably. After all, you've already been worn out by the long, arduous trip, and we won't arrive at the temple until tomorrow.'

'Like hostels, the Dingguo Temple also provides room and board for its visitors. For men of letters, a short stay in the temple is considered to be more desirable than a hostel, and more fashionable too,' Judge Dee explained. 'Well-known poets like Men Haoran and Wang Zhihuan have left behind lines they've written on the temple walls. You may not know, but some people come to the temple solely for the purpose of reading and copying the poems.'

'So you are thinking of dashing off several lines of your own poems on the temple wall, like other poets?'

'No, I know better. I've not produced a single readable piece for a long time. Any lines of my poetry written on the temple wall would end up being a laughing stock for thousands of years.

'But, far more importantly,' Judge Dee continued, 'I've heard rumors that other well-known poets have stayed at the temple, including celebrities like Luo Binwang. Hopefully, the monks might be able to tell me a little more about him and his stay. As you know, there's no telling which details about Luo, no matter how trivial they seem at first, may turn out to be crucial to the investigation into his disappearance.'

'If you insist on staying in the temple,' Yang said with a touch of resignation, 'that will be fine with me, Master. But after the flying knife in the fishing girl's sampan, after the cleaver in Hua's hut, I insist on staying by your side the whole time you're there. Things are getting increasingly sinister, and I'm so worried.'

'You're being overprotective again, Yang, but you may book two adjoining temple rooms if you wish. I don't think that will be a problem to arrange.'

Yang helped Judge Dee into the cushion-filled carriage, before mounting the horse with a jump.

'To the temple, then! Sit tight, Master,' Yang said grumpily, and he cracked his whip overhead.

The carriage started rolling along the road again, a bit more steadily than before. An invisible cicada started screeching in the woods behind them. It could not be the same cicada that was screeching in Luo's poem.

Judge Dee pulled up the curtain absentmindedly. Sitting upright inside the carriage, his back as straight as an aged bamboo pole, he soon felt unbearably suffocated by the heat. Perhaps he truly was getting too old for a difficult, intense investigation like this.

Luckily, the road was gradually becoming wider, embracing a far-off vista of the verdant mountains after the rain. The white clouds unfurled nonchalantly against the distant horizon. For a moment, the view appeared so enchanting that it seemed as if it was intent on making a profligate offering to a thankless, murderous world.

Judge Dee spotted a tiny scarlet animal jump out, fleeing along the gravel roadside. Possibly a scarlet fox. Could it have been the same fox he had encountered in another murder investigation? Judge Dee laughed at himself. That was a black fox – or a black fox spirit in surreal, superstitious imagination, and the crown prince had not been exiled out of sight at that time.

Ironically, people had been calling the empress an evil fox spirit, shamelessly wanton, cunning, shrewd and cruel, with an almost supernatural bewitching power.

But the present investigation was drastically different, with no supernatural elements. It was simply a missing-person case – on the surface, at least. Luo was still missing, but now three other persons – directly or indirectly related to the investigation – had been brutally murdered.

The most inscrutable death, and the most unbearable too, had happened the previous night, with Little Swallow's body lying on the deck of the sampan, next to him. In spite of what Judge Dee had told Mayor Qian about Dee himself having been the murder target, he knew it was not true. The assassin's knife had been aimed at her.

And that changed the whole picture of the investigation for Judge Dee.

But the question of why she had been murdered was breeding, growing into so many related questions.

Little Swallow had entertained Luo for a couple of nights, but Luo had not told her anything significant about him, not even his real name. As for the poem he'd written for her, and left in her care, it might have been nothing more than a few random lines, dashed off as poetry for the sake of poetry. The feelings he'd expressed could have been conventionally romantic poetic hyperbole. As Judge Dee had explained to Little Swallow, the allusions in the poem were commonly used among Tang dynasty poets.

Like these other poets, Luo could have simply been carried away while putting down those sentimental lines. But that was all. What was true in the poem was only true for that moment, in that place. Not to mention the ironic fact that Little Swallow was an uneducated girl, unable to read and understand poetry.

It did not take too long for Judge Dee to notice that his blue cotton gown was now drenched with sweat again. The carriage kept trudging on along the treacherous trail. He was growing old, he told himself, pushing open the paper window wider and fastening on his bamboo hat against the glaring light.

NINE

'History is a set of lies agreed upon.'

– Napoleon Bonaparte

'All the world's a stage,
And all the men and women merely players;
They have their exits and their entrances;
And one man in his time plays many parts . . .'

– William Shakespeare

'Mother, I have tried to make the far-off echo
Yield a clue to what is happening to me;
In the old palace people come and go,
Seeing only what they want to see.'

– Qiu Xiaolong

That night witnessed Judge Dee checking into a small inn to break his journey. It was quite late, and a solitary lantern outside the inn shone feebly against the surrounding darkness. Will-o'-the-wisps were abundantly visible in the rice paddy field nearby.

Judge Dee lit a medium-sized candle in the cozy inn room, spread a piece of paper out on the table and tried to make a list of possible connections.

After circling a couple of names with his brush pen, and trying to connect them in his mind, he became lost in thought.

Waves of frog croaks kept coming over from the field not too far away, irritating him. Eventually, he put down the list with a sigh. The crisscross lines he had drawn on the list of names had led him nowhere. Inexplicably frustrated and worn out, he repeatedly rubbed his temples hard against the onset of a splitting headache.

Out of the window, he could hardly see anything, just indistinct shapes. To his surprise, despite the lateness of the hour, he could suddenly hear a monk's chanting of scripture wafting over from some distance, the words barely perceptible. The chanting could not be coming from the Dingguo Temple, Judge Dee knew; Yang had informed him that the temple in question was still far, far away.

The nighttime chanting continued in a broken rhythm, off and on, along with the night watchman's melancholy, insistent knocker, which kept beating the time as he walked along the trail outside the inn.

Judge Dee pushed open the window as wide as it would go and propped it open with a small wooden peg. The night appeared to be quite advanced. The full bright moon seemed to be suspended in the deep-blue sky, as if it were resting on a gigantic black crow's wing.

A black crow was commonly thought to be as ominous as a black fox spirit, in those countryside folk tales he had heard of.

At last, Judge Dee sat back at the table. Then he began grinding a pine-smoke inkstick mechanically on the Duan ink-stone, hoping the pleasant ink smell might somehow help to clear his mind.

Life consisted of nothing but appearances, seen from one's own perspective. But was it possible for someone to step out of his own perspective, however briefly?

After a long while, Judge Dee heaved another sigh. He had spent more than an hour and a half trying to connect the dots into a recognizable picture. Reading and re-reading the poems connected to the case. Reading between the lines and decoding them laboriously. Speculating about the things that could have connected the innocent victims who had fallen in this investigation. Instead of being a simple missing-person case, the investigation was becoming more and more like a complicated, diabolical serial murder case.

He was finally putting down his brush pen, resting it on the ink-stone, when he was startled by an unexpected spark from the flickering candle. The brush pen rolled out toward the wall, leaving a light ink stain there.

Writing on the wall!

Was that another sinister omen? The investigation had been full of foreboding from the very beginning, causing collateral damage every step along the way.

Alas, who would light a candle for Ning, for Hua or for Little Swallow?

Judge Dee trimmed down the candle with his fingers, wondering whether he might finally be ready to go to bed, yet aware his mind was still churning.

He told himself repeatedly that there was another full day waiting for him the next morning.

Finally, he was just trying to close his eyes when he was galvanized by a new thought.

He bolted up from the bed and clamped his hand over his mouth, lest he exclaimed out too loud in the thin-walled room, disturbing others in the tranquility of the night.

Yes, there was something he had overlooked. Something serious, sinister. As an experienced judge, he should have been alert to this possibility much earlier.

Judge Dee himself had been shadowed all the way – for a much more devilish purpose than he'd first thought. His visits to possible suspects, in his search for clues to Luo's whereabouts, could have meant more than he'd suspected to those shadows walking beside or behind him. They'd watched him in deadly seriousness, followed him all the way from the very beginning. But instead of simply hoping to glean crucial clues from dogging the footsteps of a celebrated judge like Dee, they had been taking his suspects as their targets.

He had known, of course, that he was under constant surveillance by Her Majesty. The unexpected appearance of Minister Yuwen at the meal with his poet friends had shown that clearly. But he had thought his shadows were there for one purpose alone: to ensure he carried out the investigation into Luo Binwang's disappearance with utmost speed and sincerity.

But what if they had another, secret, mission?

What if they were there instead to find something of ultimate importance that Luo had left behind?

What if no one – even the shadows – knew what this item of ultimate importance was, except the empress herself?

Perhaps the shadows were tasked with both surveilling his investigation into Luo Binwang *and* retrieving this mysterious unknown item, Judge Dee thought. But at the same time, this parallel investigation must have far more importance to Her Majesty, because the way Dee's shadows were investigating their own case was categorically different to his. As in the Chinese proverb, they did the ultimate job by pulling up the weeds by their roots. That was why whenever a suspect was approached by Judge Dee, they hurried over, searched around frantically and then murdered the suspect in cold blood . . .

For what?

For something even more crucial than the judge had been aware of. It was more than a diabolical attempt to find Luo and get him out of the way forever. Rather, it was to get rid of something of unimaginable importance that had been in Luo's possession – and was now possibly in the possession of one of the victims.

Judge Dee was unexpectedly reminded of an ancient proverb – from as early as the Spring and Autumn period: 'You are guilty simply because of the precious jade you have in your possession.'

To put it another way, this invaluable possession could be the cause of all of Luo's current troubles. Whatever the cost, certain people lurking in the background wanted to take this item into their own possession – through murderous conspiracy, by hook or by crook, by knife or by cleaver.

The current era was a time, Judge Dee knew, when emperors or empresses were absolutely powerful, absolutely corrupt, yet supposedly endowed with a divine mandate, so people would obey their orders, no matter how cruel.

This theory – that the murders were being carried out in a desperate attempt to find something dangerous that Luo had left behind – was particularly evident in Little Swallow's case. It accounted for the second thrust of the flying knife, attached with hooks and a long line, which had been thrown out for the very purpose of retrieving the parchment in her hand.

Judge Dee drew several quick conclusions about the murder that had happened in the sampan, trying not to remember Little

Swallow bleeding, breathing her last breath, her once-vibrant body growing as cold as ice.

His first conclusion was that the knives could not have been thrown from afar. It had been near dusk, with poor visibility. They were on the river, at a distance from the bank. So, more likely than not, the knives had indeed been thrown from the black-topped sampan nearby, as Judge Dee had suspected.

His second conclusion was that, as the two knives had flown at Little Swallow in such quick succession, there must have been at least two assassins in that other boat.

And his third conclusion: whatever they had tried to snatch from the fishing girl, it must be of extreme political significance. It would have taken a lot to have such an assassination planned and executed on the very day Judge Dee had arrived at the Shu River.

So the stakes concerning what Luo had possessed must be unimaginably high – regardless of whether the item was still carried by Luo himself or by somebody else connected with him, who was possibly concealing it on his behalf.

But, Judge Dee reflected, the item so violently retrieved from Little Swallow's body had been a poem, nothing more.

Why had the assassins, lurking in the darkness, considered a love poem composed by Luo Binwang to be so dangerous to their master that they had to retrieve it? The assassins must have seen clearly it was just a piece of paper, and yet they still threw the knife with hooks and a line for the second time. It was because they could not read what was written on the paper at a distance.

Judge Dee could come to no more conclusions. Not for the moment. But what was the next step he should take? He cudgeled his brains, yet to no avail.

Perhaps it was just like another old Chinese saying. Judge Dee had no option but to wade across the river simply by stepping on one stone after another – however slippery and hardly visible beneath the surface of the darksome, treacherous water those stones might be.

TEN

'Two things fill the mind with ever-increasing wonder and awe, the more often and the more intensely the mind of thought is drawn to them: the starry heavens above me and the moral law within me.'

– Immanuel Kant

'Bent double, like old beggars under sacks,
Knock-kneed, coughing like hags, we cursed through sludge,
Till on the haunting flares we turned our backs,
And towards our distant rest began to trudge.
Men marched asleep. Many had lost their boots,
But limped on, blood-shod. All went lame; all blind;
Drunk with fatigue; deaf even to the hoots
Of gas-shells dropping softly behind.'

– Wilfred Owen

'The world is the totality of facts, not of things.'

– Ludwig Wittgenstein

It was almost noon the next day.

Yang looked over his shoulder toward Judge Dee, who was once again sitting straight-backed in the carriage.

'Look, Master. Once we've turned around the corner, we soon shall see the Dingguo Temple. You have to take a much-needed break when we arrive. Last night, I saw that the candle in your room at the inn was still lit almost till dawn.'

'As always, you worry too much about me, Yang,' Judge Dee replied. 'It will be quiet and peaceful in the temple. The atmosphere there is supposed to contribute to rest, to self-cultivation and to poetic inspiration. And it may prove helpful to my contemplation over the cases too.'

Yang did not make any immediate response to his master's

argument, having had more than enough metaphysical talk over the last several days from his pedantic master. He thought he could have guessed something about Judge Dee's dramatic metamorphosis into a poetry-addicted bookworm. If anything, it probably served as a cover for the ongoing investigation as well.

A couple of small apricot-colored banners streaming in a breeze by the roadside soon came into view, indicating that the Dingguo Temple was located in the vicinity.

As the carriage rattled round another corner of the road, Judge Dee thought he could hear a bell – or a couple of them – striking, reverberating in the air, presumably coming over from the ancient temple in question.

'So many temples in this area. A poem from the contemporary poet Du Mu is crossing my mind again,' Judge Dee said to Yang, with a wan smile.

Among the four hundred and eighty temples left
behind from the earlier dynasties,
how many of them in the south are mantled
in the mist and the rain at this moment?

'Yes, those bells must be ringing from the Dingguo Temple, Master.'

Unexpectedly, the ringing from the temple turned into a cacophony of numerous bells ringing all together. The sound seemed urgent, even panic-stricken, to the bewildered master and servant.

Poking his head out of the carriage to see further into the distance, Judge Dee caught a glimpse of the sky inflamed in the eclipsed sunlight. He contemplated it in confusion and then was hit with a shocking realization. The temple was being engulfed by fire.

'What's happening?' Yang exclaimed.

'The temple is on fire, I'm afraid,' Judge Dee responded. 'Possibly a big fire.'

Weird, inexplicable things had been happening around him since the beginning of the investigation. Judge Dee was still astonished by the discovery that he had become a harbinger of death or tragedy, though he'd not had time to elaborate on it. But so far, the deaths had occurred *after* his visit to each of these places.

This time, tragedy was occurring at the Dingguo Temple, which was being consumed by fire, before he'd even arrived.

What could that change possibly mean?

'Let's wait here by the roadside for a short while, Yang,' he said, wiping the cold sweat from his forehead with the back of his hand, feeling another wave of terrible sickness approaching. 'There is no need for us to do anything in a hurry right now.'

Judge Dee's instructions made a lot of sense to Yang, and he nodded vigorously. There was no point in rushing headlong into the temple when it was being consumed by fire. Especially not for his aging master, who was more than tired at this moment.

'What else can we possibly do, Master?' Yang began grumbling again after he'd helped Judge Dee out of the carriage and on to a pile of cushions on the ground. He spat three times forcefully in another superstitious attempt to ward off bad luck. 'That woman in the Forbidden City keeps on bringing you one trouble after another on this trip.'

The identity of 'that woman in the Forbidden City' was a no-brainer for Yang's master, and his servant's words just added to the judge's sickening sensation.

Could all of this have been a coincidence? Once again, Judge Dee had to rule out the possibility, stroking his white-streaked beard in depressed contemplation of all the possible conspiracies that surrounded the investigation.

'That woman in the Forbidden City—' Judge Dee echoed mechanically and stopped. He did not want to think about it, either.

But the question remained, staring hard at him, giving him no break . . .

For what purpose had the temple been set on fire?

Empress Wu had repeatedly compared him to a staunch pillar of the Tang Empire. To be fair to her, Judge Dee believed she was quite sincere in saying so. She trusted him, in her way. And she had chosen to dispatch him out of the capital for this special investigation into Luo's disappearance.

But other theories, particularly the one about the empress's hidden agenda, began overwhelming him.

'I have a bad headache, Yang,' Judge Dee decided. 'I'll dash off a herbal prescription – something I've learned from Doctor Hua. Poor old Hua! I will wait here while you check the state of the temple. You may then give the prescription to a nearby medicine store before you return to me.'

There often seemed to be a tacit understanding between the two. Judge Dee was capable of thinking of this or that, or a lot of things simultaneously. Yang might not be able to understand his schemes immediately, but he always made a point of playing along, without raising too many of his own questions.

Yang took the prescription from the judge's hand and inserted it into the pocket of his gown. He stood up, ready to set out on his errands.

'Another thing,' Judge Dee continued, still leaving the woman in question out of his discussion with Yang, 'do we have something like a white towel in the carriage?'

'Yes, we do.'

'Take it out and tie it tight around my forehead. That may help my headache a little. I have heard people talking about it as a headache cure, so hopefully it will also work for me.'

Yang did as he was told. It was conventional for farmers to do that in the countryside, but it struck Yang as weird to see Judge Dee turning into a believer in herbal medicine all of a sudden, an invalid sitting on the ground with a white towel circling his forehead, just like a country bumpkin. But, Yang reflected with a wry grin, a sickly appearance in a man of Dee's age would not strike other people as surprising or suspicious, after all.

Yang fetched Judge Dee a cup of fresh water from a small gurgling stream nearby. There were tiny, colorful fishes swimming in the stream, bursting out tiny bubbles in the light amid the floating waterweeds.

'You do whatever you need to do, Yang,' Judge Dee said, reclining against a gray rock by the roadside and sipping slowly at the water cup Yang had handed him. 'And you may also take a quick look around for yourself.'

* * *

Finally, the hubbub surrounding the temple seemed to be ebbing a little, though a pungent smell of smoldering timbers and burning embers remained stubbornly lingering in the air.

Judge Dee looked up again. A darksome silhouette of the Dingguo Temple was emerging out of the smoke. Probably damaged, it still stood solid, intact. He heaved a long sigh of relief.

He was then treated to the sight of Yang hurrying back from his reconnaissance in the neighborhood, wiping his sweaty face with a smoke-soiled hand.

Yang came striding up to his master, who was still reclining against the rock. 'I have taken a quick look around the temple, Master, both inside and outside. The fire was put out, but damage was done, especially in the area close to the temple's back garden. The fire seems to have started there out of the blue and spread all around in no time. Fortunately, there was no loss of life, I've just heard, but the monks and the village people are still searching and digging in the debris.'

'Fortunate, indeed. The news is not too bad,' Judge Dee echoed, knitting his brows.

'So what we are going to do now, Master?'

Judge Dee stood up, stretched himself and shook off the dust from his long gown. He took out his official business card and said to Yang, 'Let's go there now. Present my card to the abbot of the temple. You may tell him that I unexpectedly fell sick on the road, and that I would like to stay in a room at the temple for a short convalescence period – that is, if it's not too difficult for the temple to make the arrangements without notice, and if the rooms are not too damaged by fire.'

'How could the abbot say no to you? Your stay in the temple would bring a huge honor to it, Master.' Clearing his throat, Yang went on, 'Still, you're sick and exhausted from this long trip, and you need to check into a comfortable hostel, definitely not into a temple recently devastated by fire! There is still a pungent smell there.'

'No, I must stay at the temple. Rumor has it that Luo once stayed in the temple for a period, and if he did, he may have written a few poems on its back garden wall. It's sort of a fashion among the Tang literati, you know. So, I must search for evidence there in secret. If Luo has a connection to the place, it's quite possible that after the defeat of the rebellion's army, Luo could have hidden in the temple or its neighborhood.'

The Dingguo Temple was located halfway up a hill. It was not high, but it took no less than fifteen minutes for master and servant to climb up there in the carriage.

Once they arrived, Judge Dee waited in the carriage while Yang hurried off to meet the abbot.

The abbot, an old monk in his seventies whose Buddhist name was Vanity, readily agreed to Judge Dee's request to stay there for three or four days to help him recover from his headache. Yang thought the abbot did not seem too surprised by it. There was, after all, nothing unusual or suspicious about such a request from an old man like Judge Dee, whose body was suffering from the fatigue of too much travel. Nor was such an arrangement out of the ordinary for the temple.

The abbot immediately ordered a young receptionist monk, his Buddhist name Disillusion, to hurry out to the gate with Yang to welcome in the celebrated judge.

Probably in his mid-twenties, Disillusion had a square face, alert eyes and a shaven head that was as shiny as a peeled egg in the light. He looked as thin as a bamboo stick in his red, ample-sleeved silk cassock.

He bowed low and respectfully to Judge Dee. 'Our abbot wants me to apologize to you, Your Honor. But for the urgent matters piling up after the fire in the temple, he himself would have rushed out to welcome such a distinguished guest as you.'

Judge Dee got out of the carriage and stepped over the temple's threshold into the front yard. With the white towel tied around his silver hair and his brows knit, as if he were still plagued by a splitting headache, he really looked like a sickly old man . . . which was true, except for the headache part.

Even though a large section of the temple still contained smoking debris, the judge insisted on paying full price for two rooms for a convalescent period of five days. From Disillusion's perspective, the down-payment for their board and lodgings would certainly have been more than welcome, not to mention the fact that Judge Dee's choosing to stay there would further contribute to the temple's fame.

Yang grumbled in a subdued voice as he carried Dee's luggage into a barely furnished room. Its walls were slightly smoke-stained, but it proved to be otherwise clean and neat. Yang's own room was smaller, but he did not think he had any reason to complain about that.

Disillusion was still grinning from ear to ear, bowing repeatedly, as he left Dee and Yang alone in Judge Dee's room.

'For the price, you could have chosen a much better hostel, Master,' Yang complained as soon as Disillusion was out of earshot. 'How will this half-burnt temple be able to provide either satisfying service or decent meals for you?'

'For one thing, the vegetarian meals here may turn out to be good for my health,' Judge Dee said. Then he added, after a short pause, 'Not to mention the enjoyment of reading the poems on the temple's back garden walls at my leisure. In fact, I would like to go to the back garden right now for a short walk, I think.'

'If the walls are even still there, my poetic Master,' Yang said grumpily, moving back into his own room.

Possibly a large part of the wall would be gone; Yang had reported that the fire had begun in that area, hadn't he? Still, Judge Dee could, and should, take a closer look there for himself.

If nothing else, he could look for clues as to the origin of the sudden fire.

Besides, he might be able to leave a few lines of poetry behind himself on the remaining walls. It was a fashionable convention at the time, and although Judge Dee had dismissed the idea earlier, he now changed his mind as a new idea occurred to him. Leaving his lines on the temple wall could also serve as written proof for Empress Wu: the bookish judge had truly traveled a long way in search of the missing Luo Binwang.

The empress exercised a powerful network of secret police and secret spies everywhere in the empire – as far as the Dingguo Temple. If the murders that had dogged Judge Dee's footsteps so far were not at her command, after all, then he could not afford to overlook details like this at such a juncture.

Looking out into the front courtyard, Judge Dee caught sight of a white curly-haired cat napping languidly. It was stretching contentedly in its dream, purring occasionally, as if that was the one and only purpose of its feline life.

A note of eternal sadness unexpectedly streamed over in a fitful breeze from the direction of the back garden. Turning over his shoulder for a glance, Judge Dee noticed a swarthy monk steadily striking a huge bronze bell. Judge Dee must have heard the note before. But why it was affecting him so deeply right now, he could not understand.

After a short nap, and a bowl of noodles topped with wild mushroom and bamboo shoots, along with a cup of freshly squeezed fruit juice, Judge Dee felt recuperated enough to walk out into the temple's front courtyard. His decision to stay in the temple was proving not to be a bad one so far, though he was still wearing the white towel around his head, and leaning heavily on a handy bamboo cane the temple had considerately provided for him.

There was a large bronze urn for incense burning in the center of the courtyard. It might have been placed there for devoted pilgrims, who traveled to the temple from far and wide. Judge Dee paid for a bunch of tall incense sticks, kowtowed three times with the incense sticks grasped tight in his hand, before he put the burning sticks into the bronze urn.

Enveloped by the agreeable smell of incense, a new – though still evasive and elusive – idea hit him like a thunderbolt out of nowhere. In Buddhism, it was probably called 'the sudden enlightenment'.

Judge Dee spun round abruptly, heading back to his room. It must have seemed to the temple people that he was still too weak to move from his room for long, and that it would take days for him to recover.

Disillusion hurried over with concern clearly registered on his face. 'Everything OK, Your Honor? You're looking a bit tired right now.'

'I'm fine, Disillusion. I am indeed just feeling tired, so I'm going back to my room to rest a little. Don't worry about me.

By the way,' Judge Dee said, deciding not to lose any time leading up to the question he wanted to ask, 'I've heard a lot about the famous poetry walls in your back garden. Many celebrities have left their lines on the walls, am I right?'

'Yes, quite a number of well-known poets have chosen to do so. It's a credit to our temple. Only, I'm afraid the back garden is still in a mess at the moment after the fire, Your Honor. It may take a day or two for it to reopen properly . . . or possibly even longer. But I think I may be able to arrange a special private tour for you later this afternoon or tomorrow morning when the debris has been removed.'

'I see. That will be fantastic. Let me know the exact time. I really appreciate you making the arrangements.'

'Also, I'm afraid I must share a piece of bad news I've just learned, Your Honor. A couple of bodies have been discovered under debris, not far from the back garden. Alas, the two bodies were burned completely out of recognition.'

'Were they temple monks?'

'No, we don't think so. Since no monks are missing in our temple, I am told that the dead must be some penniless people who were taking temporary shelter in the temple for free. Their lodgings were located close to the back garden. Oh mercy, my greatest Buddha!'

'Take me to the scene of the fire right now, Disillusion,' Judge Dee demanded. 'I have to be there.'

'But you're still too weak, Your Honor! The lingering smoke in the area around the poetry wall may not be too bad, but the air quality is simply too horrible where the bodies were found. It won't be good for your health right at this moment.'

'But don't forget I am an investigating judge. I have no choice but to go to the crime scene – the fire scene – this very moment. It's my calling. I cannot run away from my responsibilities, you know.'

ELEVEN

'Soldiers are citizens of death's grey land,
Drawing no dividend from time's to-morrows.
In the great hour of destiny they stand,
Each with his feuds, and jealousies, and sorrows.
Soldiers are sworn to action; they must win
Some flaming, fatal climax with their lives.
Soldiers are dreamers; when the guns begin
They think of firelit homes, clean beds and wives.'

– Siegfried Sassoon

'The limits of my language mean the limits of my world.'

– Ludwig Wittgenstein

'Truth is found neither in the thesis nor the antithesis, but in an emergent synthesis which reconciles the two.'

– Georg Wilhelm Friedrich Hegel

Late in the afternoon, Judge Dee returned to his room in the temple, weariness weighing him down like a heavy blackboard which bore the characters of a person's name written on it and then crossed out. Such a blackboard would be hung around the neck of a criminal and exhibited conspicuously at the execution ground. It signified that the person with the name written and crossed out on the board was going to be beheaded soon.

Pulling his swollen feet out of his heavy boots, Judge Dee changed into a pair of straw slippers provided by the temple and heaved a sigh of relief. After making himself a cup of Dragon Well tea, he pushed the armchair closer to the wide-opening window and sat down, inhaling the light fragrance from the dainty cup.

In the distance, a gray wild goose was flying over a discolored pavilion, its wings flapping against the increasingly oppressive sky. Resting his elbow on the arm of the chair, and his chin on his fist, Judge Dee stared at the desolate scene gloomily, trying to sort through what he had learned earlier in the day.

With both Yang's information and his put together, he'd still failed to produce anything close to a scenario to account for the fire – not even something plausible enough to explain it to himself.

Nor had his examination of the fire scene in the company of Disillusion yielded anything substantial. The only new evidence he'd found was a scrap of paper, which he'd torn violently from the tight, rigid fist of a nameless body, lying charred beyond recognition near the back garden of the temple.

The scorched scrap was also a puzzle, but the bewildered judge wondered whether he could make anything of this potential clue. He could only make out two or three characters written on it – blurred, barely readable, but totally meaningless out of context.

More likely than not, it was just something like a fragment of a cherished letter from home, sent to the deceased beggar in better times.

Judge Dee turned to the table beside his chair and started grinding his mountain-pine-smoke inkstick slowly on a Duan ink-stone, circle by circle. Sometimes, grinding the inkstick rhythmically could somehow help to sooth his brain. Subconsciously, perhaps.

Moistening the starched point of a new brush pen on the tip of his tongue, he dipped it into the black ink, and wrote down a list of puzzling questions on another piece of paper.

After gazing at the list for a long time, he twirled the pen. He wanted to draw lines between them, find tentative connections, but he failed again in his endeavor.

'Confucius says, "Knowing the task facing you is impossible, you still have to try your best to do it, as long as it is the right and proper thing for you to do so,"' Judge Dee murmured to himself, his voice subdued, like a bookworm in Little Swallow's description. Judge Dee did not consider himself such a bookworm, nor was Luo Binwang, but the two of them did share some common characteristics.

* * *

In the meantime, Yang too had left the temple on his errand. After a short while, he returned to Judge Dee's room, carrying a large cloth bundle of herbs. The devoted servant was planning to boil them in accordance with the instructions from the herbal medicine store.

Having borrowed a small stove from the temple, Yang put an earthen pot of water on to boil. When the water was starting to heat, he dropped in some of the herbs, and then, after ten minutes or so, he threw in the remaining pieces. All the while, he checked and rechecked the instructions from the herbal store, fanning the stove clumsily. His forehead was deeply furrowed, as if the lines had been somehow etched in.

While Yang was anxious to prepare the medicine correctly, he was more worried about something else.

Judge Dee did not have much faith in herbs, as Yang well knew. So why would his master put on such a dramatic show of interest in them all of a sudden?

Yang thought it was out of the question that Judge Dee had learned so much from Dr Hua – after just one talk lasting for a couple of hours, with most of the time spent discussing Luo Binwang – that he was now able to make an effective herbal prescription for himself.

The steaming hot water in the pot soon started bubbling. Yang turned down the fire to the minimum and waited patiently by the stove like an old monk. The herbal liquid could boil over at any moment.

Yang believed wholeheartedly in Judge Dee. It was an unwavering principle for him: whatever circuitous route Judge Dee might take on an investigation, whether stealthily or not, things would never go wrong for Yang if he followed his master every step of the way.

An acceptable herbal smell was permeating the room when a knock was heard on the door. The abbot of the temple, a white-haired and white-bearded old man in his seventies, Buddhist-named Vanity, had come to call on Judge Dee. Following the abbot was the young reception monk Disillusion, carrying a large, vermilion-painted, three-tiered rattan food container.

Yang rose at the sight of the two monks and bowed to them

respectfully, before turning to Judge Dee, leaning over and saying in a low voice, 'I've reduced the fire beneath the stove to its lowest level, Master. The herbs have to be boiled for at least a couple of hours. So you will have to keep an eye on it.'

As if on cue, the short-billed earthen pot began purring repeatedly like a spoiled cat, with pieces of brownish herbs rising and ebbing in the boiling water.

Once Yang had left the room, the white-haired-and-browed Abbot Vanity made another respectful bow to Judge Dee, counting the beads of a sandalwood ring around his hand as he did so, then started speaking to him. 'So sorry about this morning, Your Honor,' the abbot said, pressing his palms together. 'We had such a disastrous fire, you know. Merciful Buddha blesses all the dead.'

'There's nothing for you to say sorry about, Abbot Vanity. On the contrary, I'm so grateful to you for providing me with much-needed shelter to recover from my sickness and my long, arduous trip.'

'Let me introduce Disillusion to you. He is a student of mine. He's young, but very capable in his way. If you require any help during your stay in the temple, just tell him what you need.' The abbot smiled a shrewd smile. His face, shrunk like an aged, wrinkled walnut, was somehow reminiscent of an ancient white owl, flying out of ancient history, hooting eerily deep in the black, impenetrable night woods.

'Oh I've met Disillusion,' Judge Dee said with a smile. 'In fact, he has just accompanied me to the back garden, where the fire began. He's a very capable young man indeed, as you have just put it, and he has been very helpful to me so far.'

'You surely could have chosen a much more comfortable hostel, Your Honor. So what an honor it is for you to choose us! You are such a well-known, high-ranking minister of integrity and incorruptibility. Not to mention the fact that you are highly trusted by the empress of our great Tang Empire!'

Judge Dee thought he could sense a deeper layer of meaning underneath the clichés the old abbot was speaking, but he chose not to dwell on it for the moment.

'The Dingguo Temple is so well known, Abbot Vanity,' he

said in return. 'A large number of famous people have come to stay here.'

'You are truly flattering us, Your Honor.'

'To be honest with you, my abbot, one of the reasons that I've chosen to stay in your temple is simple. I have heard that some of the Tang Empire's most renowned poets have visited and written lines of poetry on the temple's back garden walls. I just wanted to admire the wonderful poems written there. I've heard such a lot about them.

'That's why I insisted on Disillusion taking me to the back garden. The opportunity was essential for the sake of my continuous self-cultivation. Not to mention, of course, that it's so serene and peaceful in the temple, with the ancient bell evoking memories from the depths of our history that inspired the lines.'

'Yes, some of our Tang dynasty poets have indeed chosen to stay in our humble place, including Wang Bo, Luo Binwang, Lu Zhaoling, among many others. Alas, as you will know, many of the lines they wrote on our wall were damaged in the temple fire.'

The abbot seemed to be highly alert, despite his age. The moment Judge Dee touched on the topic of the poems left on the wall of the back garden, Abbot Vanity had taken the initiative to bring up Luo Binwang's name. It was, Judge Dee concluded, probably done on purpose. In the *Go* chess game – which is sometimes known as 'hand talk', or a conversation between hands – each move tests the opponent's response. If the old abbot was aware that Empress Wu had asked Judge Dee to investigate Luo Binwang's disappearance, the abbot could have prepared or rehearsed his response beforehand. The abbot's opening move probably aimed to show that he was not at all worried about questions regarding Luo.

'What a shame!' Judge Dee said, deciding not to swallow the bait in one quick bite.

So, their talk was to be conducted like a round of shadow boxing between two tai chi masters. In a shadow-boxing match, the two participants would strike a succession of poses, without physically touching each other. Such a display of skill was generally considered in traditional Chinese martial arts to be a sign of the highest level of achievement.

The abbot had shared, without being prompted, that some of the poetry on the burnt wall had been written by Luo Binwang and other poets. Judge Dee decided to consider the subtle implications of his words before he made a counter move.

Could the fire have been set on purpose simply to destroy the walls, and the two deaths here were simply yet more collateral damage?

It made sense, he reflected, that the empress would not want to have any traces of Luo's writing left on the temple walls. The poems could prove to be a continuous reminder of Luo's denouncement of her in his 'Call to Arms'. The rebellion may have failed, but writing lasts for thousands of autumns, as a Tang poet-sage had once argued. People could come pouring into the temple's back garden to copy Luo's works – generation after generation.

But was this motive strong enough for the empress to go to the effort of arranging the fire – scheming, commanding from hundreds of miles away in the capital of Chang'an? Judge Dee could not help wondering.

'What a shame!' he repeated. 'How could the fire have started, all of a sudden, in the temple?'

'I'm still puzzled,' the abbot said. 'As in an old saying, a too-tall monk is unable to touch his head for enlightenment, Your Honor. The temple kitchen was not cooking anything at the time.'

'That's so weird. Could it—'

Judge Dee's train of thought was derailed by Disillusion, who now took the steaming hot dishes out of the vermilion bamboo container in a flurry, placing them deftly on to the table. As he did so, the young monk introduced each of the delicacies to Judge Dee, with unmistakable pride in his voice.

'The Dingguo Temple is quite well known for the special vegetarian meals we serve to our distinguished guests. For today's meal, we have "braised pork in special red sauce", "super fried crispy rice paddy eels", "bear paws in lobster sauce", "unbelievably spicy and tender beef tendon", "Yangzhou-style steamed lion head"—'

'What an intriguing paradox!' Judge Dee commented, raising his chopsticks in an appreciative gesture. 'The special vegetarian dishes on the table appear to be named in connection to meat and fish. In other words, all of them are derived from the non-vegetable.'

'Well, for ordinary people, who are barely able to keep the pot boiling, it's a matter of course that they consider meat and fish to be the most desirable delicacies, whether consciously or subconsciously,' the abbot said with a frown. 'So the names of these dishes lend themselves to the culinary imagination. For the wealthy patrons of the temple, these vegetarian delicacies may serve just as an occasional change, and the meaty, impressive names on the menu may make the banquet sound more enticing.'

'That's a profound lecture on the naming of vegetarian delicacies! Indeed, what is in a name? But how is today's so-called "steamed lion head" actually made?'

'Dry tofu and bamboo shoots are minced, mixed with corn starch and rice wine, shaped into the shape of a lion head and then steamed,' the abbot said with a chuckle. 'The chef then gives a finishing touch by adding a couple of goji berries for decoration.'

'It's in imitation of a famous special in the Yangzhou cuisine,' Disillusion explained further. 'In the original dish, the chef cuts rather than minces the pork, cut after cut, to keep the meat juicy. He shapes the meat into large balls and then steams them in a special steamer.' Disillusion gestured with his hands as he spoke, in imitation of the preparation. 'Finally, you just need to add green onion and red pepper slices on top when the tasty dish is served on the table.'

'The lion head is just an appearance,' the abbot commented again, also raising his black chopsticks in a gesture of invitation. 'In our world of red dust, there's nothing *but* appearance, to which people give one name or another. Consider the name of the young man with us: Disillusion. Illusion is appearance, and so is disillusion. Buddha is in your own heart, so why bother about illusion or disillusion, this or that name?'

'So masterfully said,' Disillusion said with sincere admiration in his voice. 'And that's why our learned abbot gave me this

Buddhist name. Name is nothing, and nameless is also nothing. That's what disillusion is really about.'

Seemingly enlightened by Abbot Vanity's Zen-spirited lecture, Disillusion kept nodding energetically. He remained standing by the table in respectful attendance, helping with whatever was needed, like an experienced private-room waiter.

'You know what?' Judge Dee changed the subject subtly. It was time for his counter move in the shadow-boxing match. 'As people sometimes say, once an investigator, always an investigator. I might be a layman right now, but here I am, remaining helplessly stuck with the appearance of an investigator. For instance, I cannot help wondering how the fire started in the temple. It's the rainy season now. The fire should not have spread so fast, so uncontrollably.'

'It's an ancient temple,' Abbot Vanity responded guardedly, 'so our monks always keep large urns of water in the back garden, whatever the season. Believe it or not, that's where the fire first started. Your question beats me. As an experienced, resourceful investigator, Your Honor, you alone may be able to shed light on the mystery for a senile and slow-witted monk like me.'

Judge Dee dodged the counter attack. 'I'm totally in the dark too. And I have to admit that I'm still feeling too weak to do any investigation in earnest. At least, not for the present moment,' he went on deliberately, tapping his fingers lightly against the hard wood tea-stand. 'However, let me ask you a couple of possibly related questions first, Abbot Vanity. Has anything suspicious happened in the temple, or around the temple, during the last few months?'

'No, nothing that I'm aware of. I'm too old, you know, so I let younger monks take care of most of the day-to-day business in the temple.'

'Let me rephrase the question. Has anything unusual, or out of the way, happened *relating to* the temple?'

'Let me think,' the aged abbot said, scratching his shaven head. The sun was setting in the west outside the window, and only a dim light managed to stumble into the room. 'If anything, perhaps far more visitors than usual have come pouring into our humble temple of late.'

Judge Dee nodded, without making an immediate comment. It wasn't too surprising for visitors to come crowding into the temple. Perhaps some of them had visited for the sake of reading and copying the poems left behind by Luo. Those lines could have disappeared overnight at any point since his disappearance. And sure enough, they had now disappeared – or, to be more exact, the wall they were written on had practically disappeared.

In today's Tang dynasty, with the high expense of woodblock carving and printing, few people could afford to buy books. They simply copied out texts they wanted to keep in readable handwriting.

For relatively short texts like poems, a special technique had been invented for the purpose. Temples or gardens would display stone tablets of various sizes with the texts chiseled on them, and men of letters would press papers hard on the stone surfaces to make their copies. These tablets served well for the purpose of attracting more fee-paying visitors, and a fairly lucrative niche market had come into being. The disappearance of the poetry wall spelled a big loss for the temple.

Earlier, during his examination of the scene of the fire, in the company of Disillusion, Judge Dee thought he had noticed a grove of black stone tablets there. The wall might have been destroyed, but perhaps some of Luo's poems had escaped.

'Well, something else happened which appeared a bit unusual. Not too long before the fire broke out, a food hygiene inspection team made an unannounced visit to our temple kitchen,' Abbot Vanity went on, frowning in thought. 'The officials said it was nothing but a routine check, but they did not look into the kitchen alone. They searched each and every room – and each and every corner – of our temple, turning everything upside down and inside out. I have to say, I commend them for their thoroughness,' he added blandly.

Perhaps the old abbot too had guessed there was something sinister behind the so-called food hygiene inspection, but he refrained from saying anything too explicit about his suspicions to Judge Dee. After all, the abbot knew Judge Dee was highly trusted by the empress, and he'd never met or talked to him before.

'Yes, what a fastidious hygiene inspection team,' Judge Dee commented, seemingly undisturbed.

'Please help yourself to slices of fried rice paddy eel, Your Honor,' Disillusion cut in hurriedly, as if aware of something dangerous in the talk between the judge and the abbot. 'Our kitchen alone is capable of producing this special dish.'

Judge Dee allowed him to change the subject. 'Another secret recipe?'

'Well, guess what the eel is made of? Eggplant! It takes a lot of steps to make this special dish. We steam it, dry it, fry it, add the fish-flavored sauce and then refry it so it comes out crispy and tasty.'

'So crispy and tasty indeed. Actually, it no longer tastes like eggplant at all, Abbot Vanity,' Judge Dee exclaimed after chop-sticking one slice into his mouth, chewing with great gusto, enjoyment written on his face. 'Different texture, different flavor.'

The judge then hesitated a little, chewing another slice of 'the fried rice paddy eel' before broaching a seemingly new subject, the eel slice still rolling on his tongue.

'I have one more question for you, Abbot Vanity. You mentioned that Luo Binwang himself once stayed in the Dingguo Temple. When did he make the visit?'

'It was several years ago – seven or eight years, I think. Luo was very poor, in spite of being a fairly well-known poet at the time. We gave him board and food free, in exchange for him leaving his poems on the back garden wall. It's sort of a tourist attraction for the temple, you know.'

'So you two talked a lot?'

'Not that much, no. Luo's a man immersed in the world of red dust, whereas I, a Buddhist monk, am trying to step out of it. Nevertheless, he seemed to be a man of wide learning, touching on a variety of subjects. I'm interested in Zen. And believe it or not, he was quite well versed in Zen too. He even wrote a Zen poem on the wall.'

'I understand. I've talked with Han Shan, another great Zen poet whose work is full of deep images and sudden enlighten-ments. I've benefited a lot from my discussions with him,' Judge Dee said, putting down his cup, still brimming over with sweet rice wine. 'Now what did you think of Luo Binwang – as a poet and as a man?'

'I don't know him well enough to judge, but Luo is a man who's had many frustrations and setbacks in his life. He may have been filled with too much negative energy, and is therefore not in a position to see through the appearances of the mundane world. Success or failure, all the things and all the people under the sun are gone with the wind, insubstantially like a puff of smoke—'

'Your talk is imbued with profound enlightenment, Abbot Vanity,' Judge Dee interrupted, feeling obliged to prevent the abbot from digressing into another Buddhist lecture. 'But has Luo Binwang ever visited the temple again?'

'No, Luo Binwang has *not* revisited our temple.'

Judge Dee saw little point going on with the shadow-boxing performance, though. He suspected that the abbot sitting opposite him had been well prepared for this talk, perhaps for a long time. On the crucial questions, Abbot Vanity had made a point of responding cooperatively, yet had provided no concrete information. Nothing wrong about that, of course. But it also meant there was nothing for the judge to move on.

Why was such a deliberate performance being staged by the Buddhist abbot? What did the old monk have to hide?

'By the way,' Judge Dee said slowly, 'have you any clues pointing to the cause of the recent fire in the temple?'

'No, I have not. Did you notice anything suspicious at the fire scene, Your Honor?'

'Nothing,' Judge Dee responded. 'Nothing but a small burnt scrap of paper I pulled out of the fist of a nameless dead body. I put the scrap in my pocket, but when I got back in my room for a closer look, the scrap was already reduced to crumbs like dust.'

'Yes, it was small, and badly scorched,' Disillusion cut in, 'with only one or two characters remaining faintly readable, but totally meaningless out of context.'

'From dust to dust,' Abbot Vanity said reverently, 'oh Merciful Buddha!'

* * *

After the abbot and his disciple had left his room, Judge Dee stood up and looked out of the paper window, yellowed by time.

The long-haired, exotic-looking white cat was chasing its own shadow in the deserted courtyard, as if debating philosophically about the difference between being a cat and being a shadow. Turning to rub its back against the wall, it licked its tiny tongue in a gesture of satisfaction with life, slipped by the terrace and curled up on a wooden bench. As if aware of another eventless eventide approaching fleet-footedly, the white cat purred itself gradually to sleep once again.

There was no point disturbing Yang at this moment, Judge Dee reflected. There were so many new theories somersaulting chaotically into the back of his mind that he'd hardly had time to digest any of them. And he was still debating with himself about what could prove to be the 'right and proper' thing for him to do about it all. He heaved another long sigh.

It began to rain. Taking a small sip of green tea, Judge Dee listened to the raindrops pattering against the temple eaves. In the world of red dust, people are lost in appearances, as Abbot Vanity had just described to him – whether meeting in joy or parting in grief, believing only in the current place, the current moment.

But in this present moment, nothing appeared real, substantial to Dee, except for the tiny bells tinkling on the glazed eaves of the temple, which were ringing faintly in harmony with the rain dripping down to the temple courtyard, drop after drop in unchanging rhythm . . .

And Judge Dee felt the unmistakable wave of a real, terrible headache assailing him.

TWELVE

'Laws are like cobwebs, which may catch small flies, but let wasps and hornets break through.'

– Jonathan Swift

'But at my back I always hear
Time's wingèd chariot hurrying near;
And yonder all before us lie
Deserts of vast eternity.'

– Andrew Marvell

'The most tyrannical of governments are those which make crimes of opinions, for everyone has an inalienable right to his thoughts.'

– Baruch Spinoza

Judge Dee stepped out of his room and into the temple's front yard in the early-morning light, feeling properly rested. He took a deep inhale of the fresh air around the blue hills, and fastened a smooth, shiny bamboo hat on his head. It had just been given to him by an old monk, who was crouching amid piles of newly made hats.

The old monk cast a toothless grin toward the thoughtful judge stepping over the temple threshold, before he went back to slicing the bamboo in a thoughtless, carefree way, bending the slices deftly with a long cleaver. Judge Dee knew from experience that walking alone helped him to think from a new, different perspective. He could see a belt of green stretching out before him, meandering toward the gray horizon. The morning scene remained wrapped in light, opaque mist, though a ray of pallid sunlight seemed to be attempting to break out of the high, nonchalant sky.

As he strolled on, the tall, dew-speckled wild weeds that lined both sides of the hill trail kept glistening, like myriads of curious, blinking eyes.

Judge Dee had already caught himself yawning, and he stretched repeatedly to wake himself up, but seemingly in vain. The trail leading away from the temple was narrow and slippery, and it took him some effort to step carefully along it, but it was quiet and peaceful, with a view overlooking a verdant expanse of rice paddy field.

In the enveloping tranquility, Judge Dee heard a tiny pine nut dropping, dropping so lightly, and simultaneously saw his devoted servant Yang running out of the temple gate. He was chasing after him, helter-skelter, like an inseparable shadow . . . but not like those alien shadows who were tailing the judge in secret. As Yang's hurried steps drew nearer, a ray of light splashed on to a surprised brown rabbit crouching in the nearby field.

From time to time, a man may choose to play a role for reasons not necessarily clear even to himself. But after a while, the role starts to play him instead, whether consciously or not.

That might have applied to the approaching Yang, Judge Dee reflected pensively, who was not just an obedient servant but also a stubborn, self-declared investigation assistant and bodyguard. Yang had never once forgotten those multiple roles while walking beside his master throughout this ill-starred mission.

But it might also apply to Dee Renjie – otherwise known as Judge Dee – right now, he thought in ironic self-reflection as he trudged along the trail. He was still carrying out an investigation that was turning increasingly unpleasant.

The sound of the chorus of temple bells seemed to be wafting over to the trail, as if carried by a fresh breeze, but it did not really help to clear his head.

'I have nothing special for you to do this morning, Yang,' Judge Dee said, when his breathless servant caught up to him. He added after a short pause, 'Of course, you may prepare another dose of the herbal medicine for me at your leisure. Right now, I just want to take a long stroll around by myself.'

'Don't walk out too far, Master,' Yang said ominously. 'These hillside trails can be treacherous.'

It did not take long for Judge Dee to arrive at a junction in the trail, the path forking out in front of him.

He murmured the lines penned by Wang Bo, another one of the four most excellent poets of the early Tang dynasty: '*Helpless, the road forking in front of us*.'

So, for Judge Dee too, the question was whether to turn left or right here.

It did not matter that much to Judge Dee, though, at this present moment, at this present place. He did not know which direction he should follow in the Luo Binwang case either. Picking one would be just like tossing a coin in Daoist divination.

The decision to turn right or left also reminded Judge Dee of another classic Daoist maxim, which echoed in his mind: *No specific purpose may turn out to serve all the purposes.*

In the final analysis, what would Judge Dee's purpose turn out to be?

It was a warm day for the time of the year, and the judge felt a suggestion of sweatiness. He might as well keep walking, he thought. He hoped some new ideas for the investigation would occur to him, like a white rabbit jumping out of the somber woods.

Probably still under the influence of the abbot's Zen-infused lecture, Judge Dee took a careless right turn and continued strolling without a specific purpose.

Going over the twists and turns of the case, Judge Dee could not help feeling more and more inclined toward his developing hypothesis: that the undisclosed purpose of the investigation involved something crucial in Luo's possession – or in the possession of someone closely related to Luo.

Ning, the former Empress Wang's maid, was a possible exception. She had no direct relationship to Luo; at least nothing that Dee had uncovered so far. On the other hand, after the release of Luo's 'Call to Arms', Empress Wu could have also put Ning under close surveillance. Luo's powerful poem contained the same sordid details of Empress Wu's personal life that Ning had confirmed to be true from her personal knowledge. Had Empress Wu's omnipresent net of spies therefore drawn a connection between Luo and Ning, even if the two of them had never met?

Hadn't Judge Dee himself suspected such a connection in his investigation into Luo's influential 'Call to Arms'?

Had Empress Wu also been aware of Judge Dee's meeting with Ning? He could not tell. To say the least, however, Ning's murder had taken place less than a day after her meeting with Judge Dee. So he could not afford to ignore the possibility . . .

The hill trail appeared to grow narrower, with tall trees arching overhead, patched with colorful growths and dotted with small bamboo groves here and there. Dewdrops blinked their glistening eyes at the approaching intruder.

Without knowing how far he had walked from the temple, Judge Dee began to worry about the possibility of losing his way on the shaded hill. When he cast a look over his shoulder, however, he thought he could still catch a glimpse of the distant yellow-glazed eaves of the Dingguo Temple, shimmering in the sunlight.

To his pleasant surprise, he also saw a rough wooden bench located close to a turn of the hill trail. So there must be people regularly walking here. The area was not that deserted.

He might as well take a short break, he decided, another wave of tiredness assailing him the moment he collapsed down on to the hard bench. Propped against the bench's hard wooden back, he still felt inexplicably drowsy. He closed his eyes for a moment or two, in the midst of tiny buzzing flies . . .

Something uncanny shocked Judge Dee into wakefulness.

It seemed to him as if he was transported, all of a sudden, to view the romantic rendezvous between Luo and Little Swallow, the couple projected as a darksome silhouette against the surrounding green. The lovebirds were billing and cooing, their shoulders touching each other, their fingers interwoven, while the boat drifted in the shimmering ripples under the soft moonlight. Little Swallow was singing:

'The moon bright as frost,
the breeze soft as water,
a scene of ineffable beauty,
fish jumping in the curving lake,
dew glistening on the locust leaves . . .'

The scene then changed abruptly, and Judge Dee found himself in discussion with Luo on the very same sampan. Little Swallow had vanished out of sight, though her sweet singing of 'Bamboo Twig Song' remained audible in the pitch-black background:

'The clear river meanders
against thousands of willow shoots.
The scene remains unchanged
as it was so many years ago . . .

This same old wooden bridge,
where I parted with her,
brings no news, alas,
no news for today.'

Judge Dee was engaged in a serious face-to-face talk with Luo's silhouette. The conversation jumped between different topics.

'She's such a vicious woman – greedy, wanton, shameless.' Luo did not mince his words, taking a sip of blood-colored wine. 'And you are the one she chooses to trust, Your Honor. Still, no matter how hard you have worked in this so-called investigation, your mission is nothing but a wild goose chase.'

'A wild goose chase? I'm not sure what you mean, Luo. But let's try to change the perspective of our discussion. What if "the vicious woman" – as you have just called her – gets what she really wants at the conclusion of the investigation? I mean what meets with her hidden agenda, her real reason for launching this bizarre investigation.'

'What on the earth do you mean, my celebrated, experienced Judge Dee?'

'Let's suppose that the undisclosed, ultimate reason behind the investigation I've been conducting is to retrieve something of vital importance that's in your possession, or in the hands of someone closely related to you. If the woman in question finally obtains it, what would she do then?'

'What do you mean by "something of vital importance that's in your possession or in the hands of someone closely related to you", Your Honor? I'm bamboozled, my masterful Judge Dee. Enlighten me, please.'

'You know the truth more clearly than anyone else, I bet. And let's also suppose she comes to believe that you truly have disappeared from the world of red dust forever. Then what?'

'I'm not a wise, legendary, high-ranking court official like you. Can you do me a favor and make your enigmatic questions a bit easier to understand, Your Honor?'

'Let me put it another way, Luo. Let us suppose I write a report to the empress concluding my investigation into your disappearance, saying that you have been burned to death in the Dingguo Temple, but I managed to retrieve a small, scorched scrap of paper, which you were grasping tightly in your hand.

'And let us suppose, too, my report states that your body, discovered in the back garden of the temple, was burned out of recognition, and only one or two characters on the scrap were readable, and utterly meaningless out of context.'

'I'm more and more confused. In fact, I am overwhelmed by your wild, absurd argument. How can all these impossible fantasies be dovetailed together to make a coherent picture? There is no logic whatsoever, my most brilliant Judge Dee.'

Judge Dee thereupon launched into a more detailed narration about the course of his investigation. He told Luo about his speculations and theories, focusing on the mysterious collateral damage, so inhumanly cruel, which had followed the investigating judge from the very beginning of his investigation, starting right in the capital of Chang'an.

A short spell of silence fell over their boat, which was drifting in the middle of the river. Dead fish were rising to the surface, their ghastly turbid eyes still staring, occasionally goggling, as in a horrible nightmare.

'You're a clever man, Luo,' Judge Dee said. 'And I bet you know what I mean.'

'Well, let me take a guess at what you mean, Your Honor. You are supposing that lascivious, vindictive woman would, after hearing your persuasive theory, finally drop her search for me, without any real evidence of my death?' Luo said in an incredulous manner, shaking his head wildly. 'Why should I take your word for it?'

'Trust me, Luo. I'd also be taking a huge risk, as huge as yours. As in the ancient Chinese saying, the company of an emperor can be as dangerous as the company of a tiger. And for that matter, the same can be said for an empress – especially the empress in question.

'Yes, it may be argued that Her Majesty trusts me to some extent, but at the same time she also distrusts, and has suspected me, from the very beginning of the investigation. Sometimes I cannot but wonder what purpose I might have served to her. Simply as a hunting dog or a decoy for those victims she had suspected? This cannot come as too much of a shock to you, Luo. Her Majesty is someone capable of suspecting her own sons, of exiling them and – in whispered hearsay – of slaying them.'

'So you are saying you want to help me?'

'Not just you, but also the innocent victims who've followed in the wake of my investigation, the collateral damage. At the scene of the fire at Dingguo Temple yesterday, at least two burnt bodies were discovered. After the deaths of Ning, Hua and Little Swallow, and now the two nameless bodies in the temple, I have said to each of them, "I did not kill you, but you died because of me." I pledged to do something to redeem myself.'

'If you truly think this, the solution is easy. You can simply call it quits. After all, you don't have to push the investigation through to the bitter end, my noble-minded Judge Dee.'

'You think the empress would ever listen to me? She listens to the monstrous Monk Xue, to white-jade-face Zhangs, but not to me. As long as she believes you're still hiding alive somewhere, she will never stop digging three feet deep into the ground, and consequently more innocent victims will become collateral damage.'

'So you, too, have heard of those unbelievable monstrous scandals in her private life?'

It was a surprising question to be raised by Luo at this juncture. Could it be an unwitting admission of the nature of the "something of vital importance"? Judge Dee's mind was working at full throttle. Something in Luo's possession or in the possession of someone closely related to Luo—

There was a loud, violent, earth-shaking bang – and Judge Dee woke up with a start, rolling off the bench and hitting the ground hard. He groaned, and although his hand had been soiled in the fall, he tried to touch his neck, which was hurting like hell.

He must have dozed off while sitting on the bench, on the strangely shadowed hill, and sunk into a weird daydream.

But the dream had been so different from any others he'd had before. It had been unbelievably vivid, realistic and logical too. The various pieces of the puzzle had 'dovetailed' into a discernible picture, even though dreams usually had nothing to do with realism and logic, as Judge Dee knew only too well.

Both in the dream and in reality too, the hypothesis made so much sense to the still disoriented Judge Dee. There was a large, withered leaf stuck on his face and a trickle of drool on the corner of his mouth.

Perhaps he would have made similar points to Luo, whether he'd been in a dream or not.

The dream did not come out of the blue, Judge Dee pondered. Particularly because he had been thinking so hard about the ways and means to bring an end – and as soon as possible – to the disastrous investigation into Luo's disappearance. It was just like another Chinese old saying: *What a man is thinking about during the day comes into his dreams at night.*

Was it possible that Judge Dee had been seriously contemplating that he might conclude the case in the way he'd discussed with Luo in the dream?

No, he wasn't sure about that. That deliberately false scenario had only occurred to him subconsciously, flashing through his consciousness in the dream.

And, paradoxically, he could never have argued for concluding the case that way as clearly, as logically, when he was awake as he had in the surreal dream.

But what about the supernatural factors?

Well, Confucius says, people should not speak about the supernatural or the surreal.

Anyway, what would be the outcome of Judge Dee's argument – either in the dream or not in the dream? The judge was by no means in a position to tell.

In fact, before Luo had come up with a conclusive response, the dream had come to its unexpected ending, with the judge falling, tumbling down from the trail-side bench and hitting his head hard on the very real ground.

With or without the abrupt fall, the judge had to admit to himself, it was obvious that, for all his arguing, he'd failed to convince Luo that his solution would work.

What made sense to Judge Dee did not necessarily make sense to Luo. For that matter, what made sense to Empress Wu did not necessarily make sense to Judge Dee, either. It was little wonder, with each and every person looking at his or her own feet, judging things from his or her own perspective and reaching his or her own conclusion.

In fact, Luo had not said anything substantial in the dream. He was standing there more like a straw man, his answers mechanically echoing Judge Dee's questions.

Judge Dee stood up abruptly, shaking the dust from his long gown and wiping the cold sweat from his forehead. He was still reeling slightly in disorientation.

He started walking onwards without a destination in mind, feeling like a blind man on a blind horse that keeps galloping toward the edge of a fathomless cliff in the depths of a pitch-black night.

Judge Dee must have walked for a further fifteen minutes or so along the trail, lost in thought, before he came to another abrupt turn of the hill trail. He could hear a gurgling sound, faint yet audible, as if from a stream flowing, murmuring not too far away.

He told himself again that he should be ready to trace his steps back to the Dingguo Temple, but he kept on walking, even as he felt his energy levels sag. He had skipped the vegetarian breakfast.

Once he was back at the temple, he should have some vegetarian food, and he might be able to do some more serious thinking about the case with a new perspective. The perspective he had derived from the dream on the bench.

He knew there was one thing he had to take very seriously,

whether in the dream or not. If the investigation kept dragging on like this, there would be more and more victims of collateral damage. He could not see the light at the end of the shaded trail.

The empress had such a powerful network of state surveillance, with so many secret agents working in her interest alone. As it said in *The Book of Songs*:

All the people are the emperor's people,
all the lands are the emperor's lands.

For that matter, it was the same with an empress. *This* empress. As a supreme dictator, she had to have a heart of steel.

And it was also true that Judge Dee himself felt less and less inclined to push the investigation through to the end as the empress had ordered him. Indeed, he had to ask himself: for what end?

Whatever Empress Wu was so desperate to find out would no longer be any of the judge's business.

It should never have been his business in the first place, as Yang had repeatedly told him, right from the very beginning of the investigation.

What Judge Dee had said to Luo in the dreamland could turn out to be exactly what he would say to Luo in the real world of red dust, if the man was still alive.

And Judge Dee had to bring an end to his search for Luo Binwang in a way – any way conceivable – that would be acceptable to Empress Wu. It was a way Judge Dee had never trodden before.

Last but not least, he had to do it in a way that was acceptable to Judge Dee himself as well.

THIRTEEN

'Always assume incompetence before looking for conspiracy.'
– Niccolo Machiavelli

'Those who do not remember the past are condemned to repeat it.'
– George Santayana

'Act in such a way that you treat humanity, whether in your own person or in the person of any other, never merely as a means to an end, but always at the same time as an end.'
– Immanuel Kant

After groping along the trail for several more steps, Judge Dee found himself venturing into an even more secluded trail next to a large bamboo grove.

And, after taking several more steps again, he soon heard the sound of children's laughter, bursting out joyfully from the rustling, dancing bamboo leaves. Behind the bamboo grove, he was amazed by a partial view of a small but fast-flowing stream, its banks covered with verdant weeds and other green vegetation.

Under the cover of the bamboo leaves, Judge Dee held his breath, poked his head out and let his glance sweep over to the other bank.

There, four or five children could be seen scampering in and out of view – playing hide and seek, jumping around and singing blissfully. They seemed to be waving their hands at some water birds swimming there, imitating their call, 'Goo, goo, goo . . .'

Judge Dee jolted at the sound and watched on intently, understanding and yet simultaneously *not* understanding, why he felt so shocked.

On the other bank, Judge Dee then spotted a tall, gaunt white-haired man, half lying and half sitting on a rattan recliner. The man on the recliner could not have been able, due to the angle of his vision, to catch a glimpse of the judge hiding under the cover of the bamboo groves. At least, he did not exhibit any signs of surprise on his wan, pallid face when his glance swept over in Dee's direction.

The man on the rattan recliner somehow struck Judge Dee as eerily familiar.

He seemed stiff, as if he could neither sit properly nor lie down with ease. He kept his uncomfortable position for quite a long while under the sunlight, without making any movements at all. A ray of golden light seemed to be playing on his expressionless face.

Was it possible that the reclining man, Judge Dee wondered, was an invalid, still recovering from a stroke . . . or from a serious wound?

While Judge Dee was still watching, wondering, the children started singing again, giggling, frolicking by the water, jumping around the man lying on the rattan recliner, clapping their hands in the joyful chorus:

'*"Goo, goo, goo!"*
Arching its neck,
the goose is singing
to the high skies,
white feathers drifting
over the green water,
and red webs pedaling
in the clear ripples.'

Could the mysterious man on the other side of the stream be none other than Luo Binwang himself, teaching the children here to sing the poem?

The question crashed down on Judge Dee like a violent thunderbolt, attacking, breaking, crushing out of nowhere in the immensity of the azure sky.

Momentarily, the judge was too shocked to think or to react logically.

Judge Dee had never met Luo in person. The figure in the

dream had appeared as a dark silhouette and did not really count. The judge had studied several hand-drawn portraits of Luo, back in the capital of Chang'an, shown to him by the empress herself when she tasked him with the case.

Judge Dee even carried a small portrait with him, back in the temple bedroom, that the empress had generously allowed him to take with him on the investigation. But he had not examined the portrait since the beginning of the long, arduous trip.

Now, at this distance, Judge Dee could not see a clear picture of the man across the stream. At a second or third glance, though, he thought he noticed that there appeared to be a small scar above the left eye of the man on the recliner.

He searched through his memories for impressions of Luo Binwang from those hand-drawn portraits. While viewing them from this angle, and from that angle, searching through forgotten corners of his mind, the judge kept watching the man who was reclining stiff, motionless, almost paralyzed on the rattan recliner on the bank across the gurgling stream.

Finally, Judge Dee managed to convince himself that he saw some vague resemblance in his memory of the portraits – though not that striking, not that clear – to the uncanny apparition on the other bank of the stream.

Goo, Goo, Goo . . . The white goose arched its long neck high towards the cloudless skies, calling in leisure, swimming over the light green ripples.

For four or five minutes, Judge Dee compelled himself to see more and more of a resemblance between the portraits he had seen and the man he was watching on the other bank.

Judge Dee then recalled something else. It was rumored that Luo Binwang had been seriously wounded in the last battle fought under General Xu, the disastrous battle by the Wuding River. Without the excellent care and effective herbal medicine provided by the good old doctor Hua, Luo could have remained in a serious condition. That accounted for the reason why Luo could keep himself only in that uncomfortable half-sitting, half-reclining position . . .

Far, far away in the capital of Chang'an, the empress, too,

must have heard about Luo's stay in the Dingguo Temple, though many years earlier. It was natural for her to assume that after the failure of the rebellion led by General Xu, Luo Binwang could have run into hiding in or somewhere close to the temple. So when her shadowy spies had seen Judge Dee heading in the temple's direction as a possible part of his investigation, they must have assumed there was something they missed. It was likely that was why the so-called official food hygiene inspection team raided the temple.

As for the fire, it could have been a further attempt to kill two birds with one stone. One purpose was to smoke out any strangers staying as guests in the temple near the back garden – which could have included Luo.

And the second purpose was to erase the poems left by Luo on the back garden wall. With the wall burned down, the poems too would be gone with the wind. With so many things happening in the Tang Empire, people's memories were not long.

That also explained Judge Dee's impression during his talk with Abbot Vanity in the temple that the old monk had rehearsed his answers. Abbot Vanity could have known Luo Binwang was hiding somewhere near the temple. He had probably helped him into hiding.

Abbot Vanity would not have gone out of his way, however, to help Luo without good reason, and that motive was still unknown to the judge. In fact, Empress Wu was far from against Buddhism. The waters could run much deeper there . . .

So what should Judge Dee do right now?

One possibility was for him to try wading across the water, stepping on the wet stones, one after another, as in the Chinese old saying, to approach – to confront – the 'possible' Luo Binwang reclining on the rattan recliner on the other bank.

But was Judge Dee really up to the job?

The water was cold. The torrent was swift. He was old. Unpredictable risks were involved. Judge Dee was not even one hundred percent sure that the man on the rattan recliner would turn out to be Luo Binwang.

And what would he do next, if he did manage to reach the other side of the stream?

Even if the scenario revolving in his mind proved to be true on the other bank, what could Judge Dee possibly achieve?

In other words, what would be the outcome?

As in the dream, Dee did not think he would be able to win Luo over. The pragmatic judge knew that the idealistic poet would not cooperate with someone who was supposedly affiliated with Empress Wu.

At this moment, it was out of the question that Judge Dee could bring Luo back to the temple by force. Wet and exhausted, the judge did not believe that he would have the physical strength for the task, even if Luo was injured. In reality, he was hardly in better shape than the man on the rattan recliner.

It would be another story, possibly, if Judge Dee returned to the temple and then hurried back to the bank of the stream immediately with Yang.

By that time, however, the man on the rattan recliner across the stream could have long vanished.

And supposing Judge Dee did somehow succeed in dragging 'Luo' back to face the empress in the royal palace, where Her Majesty would be capable of doing whatever she pleased with the rebellious poet—

What then?

More victims, more collateral damage . . . perhaps even including Judge Dee himself.

He was not worried about himself. He felt too tired, too old and too worn out. Whatever might happen to him, it did not really matter.

Judge Dee was taking a couple of steps back, nervously, soundlessly, away from the opening in the middle of the grove of sharp, long bamboo leaves, when he was seized with a new idea.

His legs beginning to wobble, he caught himself sweating profusely, almost as if he were drowning.

From a distance he thought would be safe, Judge Dee looked back over his shoulder once again, towards the scene across the gurgling stream.

The rattan-recliner-ridden old man, as well as the playing, singing children by the water, had vanished from sight behind the bamboo grove, as if in a dream.

Could that have been because of the distance and perspective? It was possible.

Surely the idea that he'd been seized by was crazy? But it was still developing, expanding and getting more and more frenzied.

Clutching at such a crazy idea like a life raft . . . was he no longer worthy of being known as the composed Judge Dee?

Perhaps it was true – at least, during that undignified moment when he'd fled from the stream and the man who could be Luo Binwang on the other bank. He had to acknowledge that to himself. At the same time, he did not think he had any other options.

Edging toward a clearing in the woods, Judge Dee came to an abrupt stop, his brain still working frantically at full throttle.

Perhaps Judge Dee could claim that, after further research, he'd managed to recognize some of the blurred Chinese characters on the scrap he'd torn from the tight fist of a nameless body – matching the height and build of Luo Binwang – at the scene of the fire in the Dingguo Temple.

The meaning of the fragments on the scrap, though elusive and incomplete, would be guessed by the empress herself. Or, at least, the meaning would be suggestive to her, in the direction Judge Dee would imply.

Judge Dee knew he had to immediately put these new, plausible 'fragments' down in writing – an integral part of pulling the crazy scenario off – or his idea would just vanish into thin air.

He picked up a handy broken twig and wrote the characters down, stroke after stroke, on a small patch of sand not too far from the stream.

Judge Dee was now betting all his hopes on the probability that the empress would have heard a report from her secret police about the existence of the fragment, which had disintegrated in his hands. The scheme he was plotting was so new, so original, so full of unpredictable risks . . .

In short, it was not like any investigation Judge Dee had ever worked on before.

The story he was concocting to fool Her Majesty would not just put a stop to her desperate hunt for Luo Binwang, but was one with which Judge Dee hoped he could soon bring the whole deadly investigation to a conclusive end.

FOURTEEN

'No man ever steps in the same river twice, for it's not the same river and he's not the same man.'

– Heraclitus

'It is no easy task to be good.'

– Aristotle

'The mind is its own place, and in itself can make a heaven of hell, a hell of heaven.'

– John Milton

That night, Judge Dee began to work on a long report on his investigation for Empress Wu, who was currently far away in the capital of Chang'an. With the imperial six-hundred-miles-a-day delivery arrangement available to the empress, however, the report should reach her well before his return to the city.

The night was so quiet, so peaceful, with the bells chiming on the temple eaves, the candle sparkling by the western windows, the monks chanting in the scripture hall . . .

All of them seemed to be positively contributing to his work on the difficult report. It was a report which started from the very beginning of the investigation, when he'd bidden farewell to the empress in the imperial palace.

To Judge Dee, writing a case report after the conclusion of an investigation was like doing a review of it, forcing him to go over any unanswered questions. He knew, from experience, that writing helped him to come to terms with his discoveries, even though he also knew he would not put *all* of them into his actual report to Empress Wu.

Although he mentioned the help he had obtained from the poets in the capital at the beginning of his report, Judge Dee knew better than to say a single word about Ning. His report read as if he had never met her. Instead, it focused on the horrible deaths of Hua and Little Swallow, and the two nameless charred bodies near the back garden of the Dingguo Temple – one of which, he made sure to emphasize, was still grasping a scrap of paper tightly in his rigid, pulseless hand.

Judge Dee wrote that these diabolical murders, which happened in close sequence, at first appeared to be interconnected, as if in a sinister serial murder case. Judge Dee had crossed paths with all the victims in one way or another during the course of his investigation, so their deaths could also be seen as collateral damage. But while such a hypothesis seemed highly plausible initially, Judge Dee's elaborate analysis and interpretation concluded that there was nothing definite.

The death of the herbal doctor Hua in his poor hut could have been just a coincidence. Judge Dee went over in detail what he had discussed with the doctor, including the poem Luo Binwang had copied out for Hua. So while Hua qualified as one of Luo's close contacts, that had only been for a week or so. After Luo had hurried back to the battlefield near the Wuding River, there'd been no further contact between the two of them.

On the other hand, a tip from the local mayor claimed that Hua was an easily irritable, bad-tempered man, who often had arguments or fights with people in the neighborhood. That could have led to his vicious murder, Judge Dee concluded in his report.

The specific circumstances of Hua's gruesome death made this theory strike Judge Dee as unbelievable, however. It had been too blood-congealing for a neighborhood squabble. How could such a thing have resulted in a violent, savage end? It was said that with Hua's beheaded body lying in pools of blood, the impoverished hut looked just like a slaughterhouse. Dee did *not* want to include this in his report. But he did write that due to the extremely important assignment he was on for the empress, he'd decided not to stay on by the Wuding River and conduct his own investigation into Dr Hua's gruesome murder.

In the part he'd written about Hua's violent death, Judge Dee had not forgotten to quote Chen Tao's poem 'By the Wuding

River'. Whether the anti-war poem would make a difference to Empress Wu, who was so eager to be known as the number-one empress in China's history, he was in no position to tell, but he was deeply touched by the heart-breaking devastation those ambitious wars had brought upon the ordinary people, whether the Han or the Huns.

Regarding Little Swallow, there was something truly inexplicable about her bizarre murder. As a fishing girl, she was not rich, so that excluded the possibility of the killer going after her money. She was pretty, but there were other ways for people to approach her, like during the special sampan meal. Alternatively, he proposed as a different theory in his report, the culprit could have been a man rejected by her time and time again.

Could a repeated rejection be a strong enough motive for a vicious, elaborately preplanned killing? Judge Dee privately considered that the circumstances of her death did not support such a scenario. Plus, the murderer in question must have been professionally trained to be able to hurl a knife into the young fishing girl's throat with such accuracy.

And then, even more inexplicably, there was the matter of the second flashing, flying knife. The culprit should have been able to see Little Swallow fall on the sampan's deck, the knife glimmering in her throat, and then lie there, blood oozing around her body.

So why throw another flying knife? Not to mention the fact that it was a different knife, with the line and the hooks attached – as if it were engaged in fly fishing, with all the tackle. It was apparent that the second flying knife had not been aimed at her body, but at the piece of paper she'd just given to the judge.

Judge Dee summarized the facts of the murder in his long report, and emphasized that he had read only the first one or two lines of the poem when the second flying knife had succeeded in landing on the parchment, snatching it from the sampan and retrieving it to the murderer's boat.

In other words, he wrote, whoever had hurled the knife had been after something important in Little Swallow's possession. That could have been the very purpose of the murder. Since what

Judge Dee had read on the sampan had been the start of what appeared to be a romantic poem, the reason for its theft was totally beyond him, he concluded.

Soon after the murder of Little Swallow, the disastrous fire had then happened, all of a sudden, in the Dingguo Temple, claiming at least two more lives. The temple people were still digging and searching in the debris, so the number of casualties could increase.

One of the two badly burned bodies discovered near the temple's back garden was short, but the tall one pretty much matched the height of Luo Binwang, according to the material in the file His Majesty had shared with him before he set off on his investigation, he wrote.

Other than that, Judge Dee did not give any hints or guesses regarding the identity of the two burnt bodies in the temple. After all, the bodies had been burned beyond recognition, though he did not rule out any possibilities.

But then Judge Dee moved on to copy out in a list what he had managed to recover from the scrap of the paper, grasped in the hand of the nameless dead body in the temple.

*The diary of X**—*

*Finally, I have lived and died once as a wom**—*

*'What an insatiable bitch squirting non-s***—'*

Judge Dee added a footnote in small characters underneath the excerpts:

'One * indicates a character unreadable in the badly burned paper, but I'm not absolutely certain about the seemingly readable characters, either. Some of them could be nothing but guesswork, as I lack any context for the meaning.'

Judge Dee hadn't made them up, not all of them. Rumor had it that the first incomplete quote had been said by Empress Wu herself, still shaking in the aftermath of her sexual rapture, and then quoted verbatim in her lover Xue's seemingly not-so-secret diary. With her huge network of surveillance, covering the whole empire, she must have heard talk of the existence of such a diary, though she had chosen to do nothing about Xue so far.

As for the second fragmented quote, it *could* have been said by a deplorable lowlife piece of scum like Xue. It served as a vivid follow-up to the empress's rapturous exclamation that she'd finally 'lived and died once as a woman', as observed from the perspective of her lascivious partner in bed.

The report had reached its vital stage, and Judge Dee could only hope that his wild conclusions, gathered both by logic and by dreams, proved to be the real reason behind the empress's frantic search to find Luo Binwang – or, rather, the item of vital importance in his possession.

If Monk Xue's diary had been copied or stolen, with all their sexual intimacies documented in detail, it could have irreparably shattered the holy image of the empress and shredded the political stability of the entire Tang Empire. Consequently, Empress Wu had no option but to destroy all possible evidence of it, at whatever cost.

Based on Luo's vehement denouncement of the empress in his 'Call to Arms', it was more than understandable that the empress would suspect that, somehow or other, Luo had gotten hold of the diary, packed with confidential, highly sensitive information. That, in the judge's opinion, was a more than plausible explanation for why she had dispatched Judge Dee himself to investigate Luo's disappearance, and why she'd had the people who'd come into contact with him mercilessly removed. They could have been concealing this highly sensitive material for Luo Binwang.

Therefore, Judge Dee concluded, this was why the empress had sent her agents to shadow him all the way. She had to make sure that all possibilities of disastrous leaks from the diary would be snuffed out.

And it seemed to the empress that Luo must have had some secret access to the diary. So, whether the fragments he'd discovered in the dead man's hand were the remains of the diary itself, or just some copied excerpts, logic dictated that the hand clutching the fragments mostly likely belonged to Luo Binwang. At least, that is the conclusion that Judge Dee, a man well known for his expertise in finding hidden connections and clues, hoped Her Majesty would draw when she read the faked excerpts from the fragment.

As it appeared to Judge Dee, however, such a scenario was quite unlikely. He suspected the diary existed merely in rumor, and in Empress Wu's paranoid imagination. A lustful quote might have occasionally burst out of Monk Xue's mouth on an impulse, to be then heard and shared by the scandalized members of the court, but the monk would have known better than to enrage the over-suspicious empress by keeping a whole diary of these dirty intimacies or phrases . . .

Judge Dee put down his ink-soaked brush pen, thinking and staring at the flickering candle on the table. The bell of the temple wafted over on the breeze, undisturbed, as always.

In some way, the empress was just like Cao Cao, the founder of the Wei Empire, who had been a capable and resourceful dictator, and was posthumously acknowledged as the first Wei emperor. Cao Cao had declared unscrupulously in public, 'I would rather wrong everyone under the sun than let anyone wrong me.'

Cao Cao had believed in this maxim so faithfully that he'd once butchered a friend's whole family. After a crucial battle had ended in disastrous defeat for him, Cao Cao had been panic-stricken, in fear for his life. He killed all of his friend's family just because he overheard the head of the family say the words 'to kill'. As it turned out, the words 'to kill' had referred to the chicken in the kitchen, and Cao Cao had taken them totally out of context.

His reaction had been extreme, and he knew he was extremely suspicious, but he never repented for the mistake. That was how he became emperor. Period.

It was also the way of being an emperor or an empress. Empress Wu, in spite of her appreciation of Judge Dee's talent, did not trust him – at least not wholeheartedly. That, too, could have accounted for the shadows following him all along the path of the investigation. For the empress, Judge Dee was probably just a handy tool, capable of doing a good job, but simply a means to the end. Or like a fan in autumn that, after being used in summer, lies in the dust.

Writing this report involved a huge risk, Judge Dee knew. The over-suspicious Empress Wu was just like Cao Cao in many ways, and she was far more powerful than Cao Cao had been in the days when he ran for his life like a homeless dog.

But Judge Dee did not worry so much about himself – not at that moment. For him, the writing of the report was like a review of the investigation for himself – an opportunity to go over all the questions and puzzles he had encountered once again. Judge Dee knew clearly, however, that he had to stop procrastinating and finish up the report he had been struggling with.

'All the evidence, circumstantial or not, points to the conclusion that Luo Binwang was burned to death in the temple, along with whatever material was in his possession. So, I think I have done the job you have assigned me, Your Majesty. A satisfactory job or not, I cannot tell, but I have truly done all I could.

'With Luo Binwang burned to death, it will not do any good to keep people in unnecessary suspense about his fate, or to allow further speculation. So I am sending you this report to arrive ahead of me, and I have also decided to come back to the capital tomorrow. Of course, I will follow up with more details for you in person. I also need to return to the capital because of an urgent health issue.'

Ironically, it could be argued that, even this time, Judge Dee had done as good a job for the empress as he always did. After she'd read his conclusion, Empress Wu might be able to heave a long sigh of relief and sit in relaxation on her splendid gold throne.

Now all the information in the report was up to Empress Wu to interpret, not for Judge Dee.

More significant evidence, perhaps, had been that Judge Dee had happened to hear those children singing the poem 'The Ode to a Goose' near a stream which was not far away from the temple. But he did not include that in the investigation report, for obvious reasons. And it was, after all, just a famous poem and it could have simply been a coincidence.

The night-hour knocker came back for another round, circling the dark path around the temple. Presumably, it was the third round. Rising, Judge Dee looked up to the stars in the night sky before he seated himself back at the table, once again facing the difficult investigation report.

Toward the conclusion of the investigation report, Judge Dee had made an impassioned statement about those innocent victims whom he considered collateral damage of the investigation.

'Alas, I did not kill them, but they died because of me – because of my investigation of the Luo case. I've been feeling so guilty about it, Your Majesty. In the last analysis, their deaths are my responsibility. At least, I have to admit it to myself.'

Judge Dee had also briefly touched on his suspicions that he could have been followed by some mysterious 'shadows' right from the beginning of the investigation. And those shadows, too, could have had their share in bringing about the investigation's collateral damage, though he'd chosen to be rather vague about his suppositions regarding how and why.

It made sense that an experienced investigating judge, he reflected, should have been more or less aware of the conspiracies going on behind the investigation. If he didn't mention it at all, it could actually appear to be rather suspicious to Empress Wu.

The conclusion of the report consisted of a dramatic plea Judge Dee made on his own behalf.

'For many years, I've been fortunate enough to serve Your Majesty. Under your brilliant, wise rule, the Tang Empire has been enjoying unprecedented prosperity, and the map of our great empire has been immensely enlarged. Because of my incapacity, because of my age, I know I have failed to do a satisfactory job for you. Before leaving the capital of Chang'an to investigate the Luo case, I knew only too well about my own incompetence, but I also knew I had no choice but to do my best for you, Your Majesty.

'Now, in the course of the investigation, I've been badly drenched and shocked in the company of Little Swallow on the river, and that's in addition to the long travel fatigue and the stress of the investigation. Sure enough, I broke down the next day on my way to the Dingguo Temple and had to take a convalescent break within the temple's walls. Alas, I'm so withered, just like a yellow leaf ready to fall at any moment. It took me a couple of days to recover my strength enough to move around the temple for ten or fifteen minutes.

'So I have to ask Your Majesty for a huge favor. Allow me to retire, or failing that, to take a short convalescence period on my return to the capital.

'Afterward, when I have properly recovered – or if there are further developments in the Luo Binwang case – I will continue to serve you with all my strength, with all my dedication, with all my loyalty, like a dog, like a horse.'

Judge Dee was far from pleased with the comparisons he had made at the end of the long report, but that was the prevailing way a high-ranking judge/official wrote to the empress in the Tang Empire.

He was disgusted with himself.

Scratching at his white hair, he looked in the bronze mirror on the table and was shocked by his reflection. His hair was growing increasingly thin, and there was hardly enough to hold a bamboo hairpin.

A pale candle stood shivering to the side of the mirror, sparkling and shedding a single teardrop. Judge Dee signed his name at the end of the report.

For a long while, Judge Dee did not stand up.

He remained sitting at the desk, as if totally drained, suddenly too weak to move. He did not have the strength even to put the report into the envelope.

He could hear the brass bells on the temple eves ringing in a flurry in the depth of the night. Judge Dee heaved a sigh, finally ready to straighten up the material littered on the desk. He had spread out the hand-drawn portrait of Luo Binwang on the desk, subconsciously. It almost appeared as if Judge Dee wanted to keep on talking with Luo before sending the report to Empress Wu.

But Judge Dee was galvanized, all of a sudden.

He snatched up Luo's portrait to examine it more closely and checked it again. Yes, there *was* a tiny scar above the corner of Luo's left eye in the portrait. The scar Judge Dee thought he'd seen above the left eye of the invalid who'd been half sitting, half reclining across the stream.

So Judge Dee could tell himself that there was no doubt left about Luo Binwang being still alive, albeit a half-paralyzed, elderly man. He could also tell himself that if it *was* Luo Binwang, there was not much risk of his deception being uncovered by the empress. The secret police, despite all their efforts, had been unable to find Luo, and if the empress believed his report, she would order them to stop looking. Besides, Judge Dee did not think Luo would survive for too much longer.

He finally put the case report to Empress Wu into the envelope. Coincidence or not, Judge Dee had already signed his name, and he did not want to think about it anymore.

EPILOGUE

'There are *more* things in heaven and Earth, *Horatio*,
Than are dreamt of in your philosophy.'

– William Shakespeare

'The wind is rising! . . . We must try to live!
The huge air opens and shuts my book: the wave
Dares to explode out of the rocks in reeking
Spray. Fly away, my sun-bewildered pages!
Break, waves! Break up with your rejoicing surges
This quiet roof where sails like doves were pecking.'

– Paul Valéry

'Whereof one cannot speak, thereof one must be silent.'

– Ludwig Wittgenstein

To the surprise of the monks in the Dingguo Temple, Judge Dee announced his decision – without any notice – to leave early in the morning.

Abbot Vanity hurried over, stroking at his white beard, and at Judge Dee's gesture, the abbot seated himself opposite. Before the abbot could begin to say anything, however, Judge Dee started:

'I hardly slept a wink last night. My body is aching all over with a fever, and I feel totally drained.'

'I'm so sorry to hear that, Your Honor. But how do you come to be feverish, all of a sudden?'

'Perhaps I walked out too far yesterday, Abbot. Lost in the woods, I had to grope around for a couple of hours like one possessed. I went as far as a small gurgling stream with tall bamboo arching overhead. On the other side of the bank, I saw several kids playing and singing the song "Ode to a Goose" beside a half-paralyzed old man lying on a rattan recliner.'

'Really!' Abbot Vanity exclaimed, and he jumped up in shock.

It was a reaction quite unexpected of the aged abbot, who usually carried himself with an undisturbed composure, but Judge Dee thought he could guess why. It was because of his mentioning the song 'Ode to a Goose' and the half-sitting, half-reclining old invalid on the rattan recliner. It confirmed his suspicion that the abbot definitely knew something about Luo staying in the vicinity.

'You must have walked too far, Your Honor,' Abbot Vanity said in a still slightly tremulous voice. 'In fact, I don't think I can remember having ever seen such a stream shaded by bamboo groves. I have lived all these years here, you know.'

Apparently, the abbot was trying to pull himself together, ready for another round of shadow boxing, but Judge Dee did not see any point in playing along with the old monk. He thought he had already received his confirmation in the abbot's fluster.

Judge Dee just wanted to give the abbot another push, like *hand-pushing* in tai chi.

'It happened to me like a hallucination, Abbot Vanity. For a fleeting moment, I even thought I knew the old man lying still on the rattan recliner.'

'Appearance or hallucination indeed, Your Honor. Buddha show mercy on us! Everything is possible, but not pardonable.'

That sounded like another confirmation by the abbot regarding the identity of the old man on the rattan recliner.

'Yes, everything is possible, but what we do is not necessarily pardonable in the history behind us. You have put it so masterfully, Abbot Vanity.'

Luckily or unluckily, other monks also hurried over and raised objections against Judge Dee's plans for an imminent departure even though he was sick.

'I'm so sorry about this,' Judge Dee said in earnest. 'I received an urgent message from Her Majesty last night. So I have no choice but to hurry back to the capital of Chang'an. I really appreciate, from the bottom of my heart, all the things you have been doing for me in the Dingguo Temple. They have been the kindest deeds that have happened to me. Indeed, you have all been taking such marvelous care of me.'

Some of the senior monks were well aware of Judge Dee's potential involvement in fierce politics at the highest level in the Forbidden City. They only made a half-hearted attempt, therefore, to push the judge to stay a couple of days longer in the temple.

Consequently, without further ado, specially prepared snacks and freshly squeezed juice were being moved from the temple kitchen into the carriage in a hurry.

Monk Disillusion bustled around, adding this or that snack enthusiastically, and even Abbot Vanity helped with preparations.

Yang stood aside, whistling, without making any comments. No decision made on the part of his master would have been too surprising to him, though Yang thought he had heard nothing of an urgent message from the empress the previous night. He had only observed that Judge Dee's room was lit late, and he'd observed a silhouette against the time-yellowed paper window, still writing long after midnight.

Yang knew better than to raise any questions at the moment.

Nodding, Yang then mounted the carriage horse in the front of the temple and cracked his whip.

The carriage horse neighed abruptly, and Yang looked ahead of him. The road, covered with melting frost, stretched into the distance, where verdant peaks joined the still-gray horizon.

The carriage started rolling down the hill. Sitting inside, Judge Dee made no comment, either.

As it seemed to him, there was no point trying to explain to Yang what had happened the previous day and night. In fact, Judge Dee hadn't reached his 'conclusion' until well past midnight – or, rather, the conclusion as expounded in the report on the investigation to Empress Wu. Knowledge about all the political conspiracies going on behind the investigation would do Yang no good. Nor could Judge Dee have explained all this simply in a couple of sentences.

Besides, Judge Dee himself remained bewildered, in some ways, about all the conspiracies going on in the investigation.

In his mind's eye, the dream scene of his talking and arguing with Luo Binwang in the sampan on the Shu River suddenly became juxtaposed with the subsequent dream-like scene he had witnessed across the stream the previous day. It appeared as if there were no longer any clear-cut lines for Judge Dee to divide fantasy, hallucination, reality and logic.

The world, with its ever-changing appearances, seemed to be revolving faster and faster, crazier and crazier. Judge Dee merely wanted to sit tight in the rolling, rumbling carriage, with all the thoughts banished from his overburdened mind, banished from the world of red dust.

But his attempt at peaceful mediation failed. It failed to work for him right now. According to a popular Buddhist saying, appearance comes out of the heart in confusion. And his heart had still been shaking in confusion with the violent turmoil of the last few days.

He'd have to find a different way to calm down, Judge Dee contemplated, stroking his gray beard.

'The way can be named, but not in the ordinary way,' he said inaudibly to himself, repeating the well-known quote from the *Daodejing*, though it sounded like a cryptic truism.

Earlier in the investigation, Judge Dee had also restudied a Daoist maxim in that famous classic by Laozi. 'Doing nothing is doing everything.' In Judge Dee's understanding, 'doing nothing' could mean, among other things, that a man should not go out of his way to do something with a fixed purpose, but he was not too sure about his understanding of the Daoist maxim.

Could the purpose of things, like the appearance of things, have also kept on changing: this moment, like a white cloud, and the next moment, like a black dog?

The original purpose at the beginning of the Luo Binwang investigation had proved – for Judge Dee himself at least – to be utterly different at the conclusion of the investigation.

During their lunch break on the third day of their trip back to the city of Chang'an, Judge Dee and Yang chose to sit in a shady spot overlooking a small lake, sipping at freshly squeezed fruit juice and munching steamed buns stuffed with vegetarian delicacies. All of these had come out of a rattan snack basket specially prepared by the monks in the temple kitchen.

An oriole could be heard twittering nearby, though it remained hidden somewhere in the small wood. Judge Dee let his glance sweep over the lake and rest on a line of mounds of fresh soil, which had been hurriedly heaped up on the other side of the lake.

In front of the mounds stood several newly painted white wooden tablets stuck in the hard soil. Somehow, they looked like makeshift tombstones erected there for the deceased. Young weeds were sprouting on the new graves, while bubbles produced by wriggling creatures burst in the lake's green water.

Tombstones for Ning, Hua, Little Swallow, plus two nameless burnt bodies in the Dingguo Temple – had Judge Dee ruled out the possibility of one of them being Luo Binwang?

He could simply be hallucinating again as he looked across the expanse of water, Judge Dee knew. In accordance with the *Diamond Sutra*, there is nothing but appearance that fills the immense void of nothingness between heaven and earth.

In the end, Judge Dee told himself again, he'd finally come to know that he knew nothing.

A whiff of breeze ruffled the sweeping willows across the lake. He jumped up, startled at the sight of a white goose emerging out of nowhere, gliding over the deep green water in leisure. With its red webbed feet pedaling non-stop in the clear ripples, it looked as if it would reach the other side of the lake soon, bidding its farewell to Judge Dee.

Judge Dee shook his head violently. It could have been just another elusive appearance. Of late, he had frequently found himself transported away in fitful trances. He was getting old – too old and helpless to serve as a competent judge.

But he found himself seized, at the same moment, by an inexplicable impulse to put down several lines of poetry. His own lines. It was almost an absurd impulse, he knew.

Was it because Judge Dee had been mixing lately with a number of poets, or with their poems, like those poems composed by Luo Binwang, Jiong Yang, Wang Bo and Lu Zhaoling? Even a couple of them by Empress Wu, in addition to all the poets at the farewell party in the capital in the very beginning of the investigation of the Luo Binwang case.

Also, poetry lovers like Dr Hua, Little Swallow, Abbot Vanity . . . The list could go on.

So the poem Judge Dee was composing, paradoxical as it might seem to be, could actually serve as a sort of catharsis for himself, at the 'conclusion' of his investigation of the Luo Binwang case.

With the lines pedaling across the surface of his mind, singing, Judge Dee picked up a broken twig, with a surreal sensation of déjà vu, and put the lines down on a small patch of sand by the lake.

It was a patch of sand he had not seen before.

Farewell to a Goose

Across the Han Dynasty bridge,
under the Tang Dynasty sun
we are going to part, like
the plum blossom unfolding out
in a white paper fan, like
the distant horizon sinking
on a black crow's wing,
as the weeds start swinging,
unexpectedly, to an unfamiliar tune.
Bubble of wrigglers
bursting on the green water.

It was not a poem characteristic of Judge Dee's style. It was both a farewell to the goose and to the people he had encountered in the course of the investigation – some of them already dead, with weeds already sprouting on the new mounds of their graves.

How had the lines come rushing into his mind, all of a sudden? Lines somberly melancholic and sentimental, yet nonetheless full of intensity under the light of the present moment, which is already fleeing into the past moment.

Judge Dee heaved another disconsolate sigh, feeling as if the poem had been composing him, from beginning to the bitter end.

POSTSCRIPT

In my first Judge Dee book, *The Shadow of the Empire*, I acknowledged my indebtedness to Robert van Gulik's *Poets and Murder.* I also touched on Gulik's failure to resist the temptation of pulling together Judge Dee (Di Renjie, 630–700), the most famous investigating judge in the Tang Empire, and the celebrated courtesan poetess Yu Xuanji (844–871), into the most sensational murder case in the Tang dynasty. Gulik did that at the expense of anachronism. He was such a profoundly learned, encyclopedic Sinologist, that it was out of the question that he'd simply overlooked the 200-year time difference between the two main characters.

As an ardent admirer of Gulik, I too failed to resist the temptation of presenting Yu Xuanji and Judge Dee together in *The Shadow of the Empire*, a novel inspired by Gulik's *Poets and Murder*, though my Judge Dee investigation has a totally different storyline. For a far-stretched self-justification, should I have the nerve to call it a stroke of poetic or fictional justice?

In Tang history, however, there was a real case concerning Luo Binwang (626–687?), Wu Zetian (624–705), and Judge Dee (Di Renji 630–700). The Luo Binwang case was far more crucial and influential in the subsequent political development of Tang dynasty history. It was also full of complicated, intriguing conspiracies in the cut-throat power struggle at the very top of the Tang Empire. For reasons beyond me, Gulik chose not to pick that case up for an installment in his celebrated Judge Dee series.

So, all this conveniently comes into my second installment of the Judge Dee investigation, *The Conspiracies of the Empire*. And fortunately, the present book succeeds in avoiding the anachronisms of the previous book.

It is necessary for us, I believe, to take a quick look into the historical background of the three main characters: of their paths crossing one another at a given historic moment, and of their complicated relationships.

Wu Zetian was born in 624 in Lizhou. She grew up in a middle-class family with a decent education. When she was fourteen, she was selected to enter the imperial palace as a 'palace lady', to serve the first Emperor Taizong of the Tang Empire. It was said that Wu was summoned to Emperor Tuazon's bedchamber time and time again until his death in 649.

Following the conventions of the time, she was then sent to a convent, to live in seclusion as a nun for the rest of her life. She soon started a scandalous affair there, however, with the new Tang dynasty emperor, Emperor Gaozong, and she lost no time finding her way back into the palace.

In her attempt to monopolize his affection, she clashed with Empress Wang, resulting in a series of rumored conspiracies. The most significant of these was that when her infant daughter died in the crib, she convinced Emperor Gaozong that Empress Wang was responsible for the death of the baby. Emperor Gaozong therefore deprived Wang of the title of empress and promoted Wu to the empress position instead. Emperor Gaozong officially announced Wu as the empress in 655.

So, Empress Wu turned into the most powerful and influential woman at court, with the Tang Empire reaching the peak of its glory. More decisive and proactive than her husband, she presided over the court together with the emperor, coming into total control of the throne after Emperor Gaozong's death in 665.

It was difficult for a woman to maintain power in ancient, Confucianism-dominated China, but she proved to be a capable and competent ruler. She made intelligent decisions that brought the Tang Empire to levels of unprecedented prosperity. During her reign, Empress Wu expanded the borders of the empire by conquering new lands. She also helped to improve the lives of the peasants by lowering taxes, building new public works and improving farming techniques.

On the other hand, Empress Wu managed to achieve all this by employing the empire secret police – with an iron fist – in omnipresent surveillance over the Tang officials and people.

There was another reason she was capable of keeping power

in her hands for so long. It was because she succeeded in gathering under herself a group of competent and talented people, whom she promoted to top positions in court in accordance with nothing but their abilities. Among these talented people, Judge Dee cut a most prominent figure.

Judge Dee (Di Renjie), the protagonist of *The Conspiracies of the Empire*, was born in 630 in a bureaucratic landlord family. He studied hard at a young age and passed the civil service examination early, with flying colors. He had a long official career, and because of his competence and integrity, he got one promotion after another in his official career.

Judge Dee was not a judge, however, in the present-day sense of the word. Simply, there was no separation of executive and judicial powers in the Tang Empire. (For that matter, there is still no separation of the powers in today's China. The interests of the Chinese Communist Party are always placed high above the law. The current Chinese 'emperor' has had China's constitution changed into one with no term limit, to allow him to rule forever just like an emperor.) As a matter of fact, Judge Dee was a high-ranking minister during Empress Wu's reign, working in a number of senior official positions, and serving as her premier official more than once. 'Judge Dee' was a neutral title, which sounded acceptable to those involved in the cut-throat power struggles at the very top of the Tang Empire – and proved as acceptable to Judge Dee himself, too, what with Empress Wu's reliance on him, and with the high expectations the other Confucianists-turned-officials had of him.

It was said that one day, Judge Dee needed to report to Empress Wu about something urgent concerning the welfare of the Tang Empire. Rather than making him wait, she rushed out of her bedroom, her feet bare, her hair disheveled, to discuss the issue with him for hours. It was commonly believed that the empress did so to purposely imitate the first Han dynasty emperor, who was known for his successful reign, particularly regarding his sincere respect for his talented, wise officials.

While beholden to the empress for her appreciation of him, Judge Dee himself was also a Confucianist-turned-official. That spelled a deep contradiction in him. From an orthodox Confucianist stance, he was supposed to support the Li family staying in line on the throne, but at the same time, he was also supposed to support Empress Wu, who had an ambition to found an empire of her own, with the Wu family members as the successors to the new empire.

Judge Dee found himself in a dilemma, but he was not afraid to speak his mind. He told Empress Wu that it was necessary to keep the Lis in line for the succession of the Tang Empire. He based his shrewd argument on a Confucian convention – that is, only the sons or grandsons are legitimate to present the ancestral offerings to the deceased at the tomb-sweeping holiday, but not the nephews or nieces. It was an argument not well received by Empress Wu. She demoted Judge Dee to a lower position, but after only a short while, she called him back to several senior positions at the court, where he continued to serve directly under her.

The poet Luo Binwang was born in 626 in Yiwu County (nowadays Yiwu in Zhejiang Province.) At eight years old, he had already become known for his poem 'Ode to a Goose', so expectations for his career and prospects were high.

Luo's entanglement with Empress Wu could be described, paradoxically, as a matter of misplaced Yin and Yang. For an eight-year-old prodigy credited with 'The Ode to a Goose', Luo succeeded in the high-level civil service examination fairly late in life. As a brilliant, proud poet, he could not have helped complain about the unfairness of the civil service examination system under Empress Wu. What's more, after he had finally passed the civil service examination and become a low-ranking official at the court, he was soon thrown into prison for something he did that displeased Empress Wu. He was promptly released, but he must have known that his official career was pretty much doomed.

Then, as luck would have it, an unsuccessful rebellion led by General Xu Jingye in the early Tang Empire put the three of them – Judge Dee, Empress Wu and Luo Binwang – in a deeper, more intricate entanglement with one another.

* * *

So a few words about the rebellion launched by Xu Jingye is also needed here. Xu Jingye (died 684) was a Tang military general and politician, and a grandson of a famous Tang Dynasty general Li Shiji. After Emperor Gaozong's death in 683, he was succeeded by his son Li Xian, known as Emperor Zhongzong, but the actual power remained tightly grasped in the hands of Empress Wu – now the Empress Dowager. In spring 684, after the new emperor showed some signs of independence, she deposed him and reduced him to the title of Prince of Luling, replacing him with his brother Li Dan, the Prince of Yu, as Emperor Ruizong.

This move allowed her to wield even more power. It was she, not Emperor Ruizong, to whom all the officials reported their work, kowtowing under the golden throne. Emperor Ruizong had no power at all to take care of things at the imperial court.

It was understandable that some members of the Li imperial clan were distressed at Emperor Zhongzong's removal, and dreaded possible future developments under Empress Wu's rule. More alarmingly, Empress Wu started talking about founding a different empire, one called the Zhou Empire instead of the Tang Empire.

It was at that historical conjuncture that General Xu Jingye was demoted, together with a group of people closely affiliated with the Li family. There were various accusations, which appeared to be ungrounded and unjustifiable in historical accounts.

In 684, General Xu Jingye gathered those people around himself, ready to rise in rebellion against Empress Wu. Among them was Luo Binwang. He too had been demoted from his position as a secretary at the county government of Chang'an County (one of the two major counties making up the capital Chang'an) to that of a much smaller county with hardly any political significance.

Frustrated over their demotions, they started the uprising in the name of 'Emperor Zhongzong's Restoration'. General Xu Jingye mobilized the troops in Yangzhou and declared the restoration of Emperor Zhongzong's era name. Instead of letting people view it as a rebellion, he wanted to convince the people that it was a rally for the worthy, justifiable cause of the Tang Empire.

He quickly gathered over a hundred thousand men in about ten days, and he also asked Luo Binwang to draft a poetic 'Call to Arms', to convince more people to join in. It was said that Luo's composition, which laid out the reasons the uprising was necessary, succeeded in winning even more people over, the numbers growing with astonishing momentum.

After several victorious battles that took place in the initial stage of the uprising, however, the military situation changed dramatically overnight. Losing one opportunity after another, General Xu's forces were irrecoverably defeated. General Xu and his close associates fled away helter-skelter, planning to head out to the sea, and then to the Korean Peninsula, but they were intercepted and killed.

What happened to Luo Binwang, however, turned into one of the most controversial mysteries in the Tang dynasty. There were several different versions of the story. According to *The Old Tang History*, Luo was killed along with other participants in the unsuccessful uprising, but according to *The New Tang History*, which was composed later with a lot of new, and more reliable, material, Luo ran away after the rebellion ended with a whimper. It was possible that Luo's body was not discovered, decaying in a forgotten corner of the battlefield, but it was also possible that Luo ran away, managing to keep himself hidden somewhere unknown.

Anyway, after the failure of General Xu's rebellion, it was understandable that Empress Wu was anxious to find out whether Luo was killed or was in hiding. She made a show of being eager to search for a talent like Luo, but no one could tell the ulterior agenda behind the investigation. Luo was no longer a threat to the empress, so why such a frantic search?

The empress was incapable of bearing the suspense for very long. So it was logical for her to dispatch Judge Dee, her most capable investigator, to look into the mystery.

As I mentioned earlier in the postscript, Judge Dee exhibited an ambivalent stance toward the cruel struggle for power between the Wu section and the Li section at the top of the Tang Empire. Nonetheless, he'd made a courageous suggestion to the empress at the court, arguing it was imperative to keep the Lis in line for the succession. He was seen by people as a pro-Li intellectual and official, but he remained loyal to Empress Wu, working in her interests.

Judge Dee could not but have had similar ambiguous feelings toward the fight between General Xu's rebellious army and Empress Wu's forces. Not to mention the additional factor that, as a lesser poet, Judge Dee might well have had sympathetic feelings toward Luo Binwang, a brilliant poet with such ill-starred luck, and more pressing anxiety about the collateral damage caused by the investigation into his disappearance.

So, Judge Dee had no choice but to end his investigation with a conclusion not that convincing even to himself.

In the history books, of course, Luo Binwang's fate was not uncovered by Judge Dee. Theories about Luo Binwang's fate after the failed rebellion roughly fall into two main versions: Luo was killed or Luo ran away. The second version somehow became more popular, with a number of variations on the theme.

One such version recorded in official Tang dynasty history states that, in 705, Emperor Zhongzong came back to the throne, with Empress Wu finally relinquishing her grasp on power. One of the first things the new emperor did was to issue an imperial order throughout the empire to collect Luo Binwang's poems for posterity. It was commonly seen as a lame excuse to search for the still-missing Luo. After contacting Luo's friends and relatives and searching all over the country, Emperor Zhongzong's efforts drew a blank, but more and more people became inclined toward the idea that Luo Binwang was not killed at the end of the tragic uprising. Emperor Zhongzong must have had information from his own surveillance channels to make him believe so.

Speculation about this Tang dynasty mystery continues in China among academics who study that period of history. Professor Luo Xiangfa of Zhejiang Normal University, allegedly a descendant of Luo Binwang after more than a thousand years, has done a special study of the issue. The theory that Luo Binwang survived is eloquently supported by Professor Luo in his analysis of a poem titled 'Lingyin Temple' by Song Zhiwen, an early

Tang dynasty poet (655–712), who was actively writing in the same period as Luo Binwang.

The poem is about a night Song Zhiwen spent in the well-known Lingyin Temple in Zhejiang Province. It was the convention among classic Chinese poets to write lines of poetry after visiting a well-known historical tourist attraction. The first couplet of his poem reads like this:

The flying-over-peak verdant in the high mountains,
the dragon palace locking in the solitude.

'The flying-over-peak' was so called because a celebrated Indian monk had exclaimed at the sight of the peak, 'Oh, it must have flown over from India. It looks exactly the same.'

According to some historical records, Song Zhiwen wrote the first couplet but did not know how to go on, in spite of repeatedly racking his brains. It was then that an old, white-bearded monk suddenly appeared out of the blue, standing behind Song and reading out the second couplet for him in a sonorous voice:

'The pavilion overlooks the sun rising over the sea.
The temple gate faces the roaring tide in Zhejiang.'

The mysterious monk then vanished into the surrounding darkness, but the couplet instantly elevated the vision of the whole poem. It would have taken a poet of Luo Binwang's caliber, as argued by a number of poetry critics at the time, to come up with such a masterful couplet – so could he have been the mysterious monk in question?

Those critics held fast to the theory that Luo Binwang was hiding in the temple and had helped Song with the poem. Stylistically, the sensibility and diction of the second couplet do mark a huge difference from those of the first couplet.

Another clue ferreted out by Professor Luo is even more convincing, more credible. It originated from essayist Zhang Zhuo's *Anecdotes at the Court and in the Countryside*, a well-reviewed collection that is often quoted in serious Tang history works. According to the collection, General Xu Jingye was betrayed, all of a sudden, while mooring by Zhoushan at night. In the chaos, General Xu's close associates jumped into the water. Some were drowned, some were killed and some escaped. And as Luo Binwang's name was not mentioned as one who was drowned or killed, logic dictates that he must belong to the last group – those who escaped.

That theory was further backed up by another Tang dynasty scholar named Xi Yunqing, who wrote the preface to the second edition of *The Collection of Xu Jingye*. It was a project endorsed, in a sense, by Emperor Zhongzong, to whom Luo Binwang had actually done a great favor. The 'Call to Arms' rallied people to the emperor in the uprising and, years later, made it eventually possible for his reign to be gloriously restored. So Xi Yunqing understood that the new emperor wanted him to carry out the assignment in all seriousness. He laboriously did much research and collected a lot of new material into Luo's disappearance, to enable him to rewrite the preface.

In the original preface to the collection, Luo Binwang was said to have been killed by the Tang royal army at the end of the rebellion, but in the revised preface – a much longer one – Luo Binwang was said to have successfully escaped after the disastrous failure of the uprising. So the significant change spoke volumes about Luo Binning's ending, enveloped by the historical, political, cultural mist.

Another Tang dynasty poet's lines could be applied to Judge Dee at the end of his investigation of Luo Binwang's case:

Alas, the gray clouds are obscuring the sun,
I'm getting so worried, unable to see
the great capital of Chang'an in the distance.

There was no transparency at all in the great, glorious Tang Empire. Everything was clouded and couched in these sinister, scandalous conspiracies of the time.

China changes, China does not change, as I said at the end of my first Judge Dee investigation, *The Shadow of the Empire*, and I still have to say so today for the second Judge investigation, *The Conspiracy of the Empire.*

In fact, the Italian philosopher Benedetto Croce put it so well: 'All history is contemporary history.' That means history is written from the point of view of contemporary preoccupations.

So is *The Conspiracies of the Empire*, at least to a fairly large extent. This historical novel by a Chinese-born American author, written in contemporary times, cannot claim to be an exception from it.

In the light of Benedetto Croce's brilliant observation, we may come to find it far from surprising that Chairman Mao wanted Chinese people to sing the praises of ambitious emperors in Chinese history, such as the first Qing dynasty emperor, the Han dynasty warrior emperor, the first Tang dynasty emperor, and the first Song dynasty emperor. He did not mince his words in his poem titled 'Snow'.

And it's little wonder, too, that during the Cultural Revolution (1966–1976), Madam Mao wanted Chinese people to sing the praises of Empress Wu of the Tang Empire. It was to pave the way for Madam Mao to eventually become a red empress after Mao's death. And the current would-be emperor in contemporary Beijing's Forbidden City not only has had China's constitution changed to clear his way to the 'throne', but also wants people to sing the praises of the first Qing dynasty emperor, with a newly made TV series extolling that Qing emperor and his grand achievements to the skies.

Such an 'emperor complex' deeply worries me. It is an apparition of a complex that has haunted China's history for thousands of years. All the leaders of peasant uprisings from time immemorial in China, if successful, ended up becoming emperors of different empires. There's no exception. Not to mention the historical fact that the first president of the Republic of China, Yuan Shikai, almost immediately attempted to reinstate the monarchy and named himself the first emperor of the Empire of China, though his reign was short-lived. Ironically, Chinese netizens have nicknamed the Forbidden City's current emperor 'Yuan the second' or 'Yuan the idiot'. The Chinese character *er* could mean both the 'second' and 'idiot'. Hence, Yuan Shikai becomes too sensitive a word, which can cause an online blog to be removed instantly, with all the 'net cops' keeping airtight surveillance. So to call attention to this serious issue is the least, I think, I can and should do in *The Conspiracies of the Empire*.

Back to Benedetto Croce's insightful observation: 'All history is contemporary history' – that is, history is written from the point of view of contemporary preoccupations. Much as I admire Robert van Gulik's historical novels, I cannot but have my point of view of contemporary preoccupations.

And Judge Dee is living in the moment of the great Tang Empire that Du Fu described.

Lost in the sentimental recollection
about the long history of a thousand autumns,
I'm shedding my tears in profusion:
The different dynasties, the same melancholy.

APPENDIX

Here is a group of selected poems by the 'four excellent poets of the early Tang dynasty' – Luo Binwang, Jiong Yang, Wang Bo and Lu Zhaoling. As poets, they were active around roughly the same period. Some of Luo Binwang's poems, or parts of poems, already included in the text of the present mystery, reappear in this appendix. I hope the translation of these poems might make it a bit easier for readers to understand their comprehensive, complex poetic as well as linguistic sensibilities, and to understand their background in Tang Empire culture and politics too. (Poetry translation is, of course, an impossible mission, but for this book in the Judge Dee series, I have tried my level best.) After all, the development of *The Conspiracies of the Empire* hinged on Luo Binwang's poems, which provide the essential clues for Judge Dee's investigation.

Also included are a couple of pieces by Empress Wu, including one about her 'incestuous' affair with Emperor Gaozong, and one about her appreciation of Dee as a high-ranking official. Ironic as it may seem, Judge Dee had only one – mediocre – poem, left behind in *The Complete Poems of the Tang Dynasty*. It was written to commemorate the occasion he accompanied Empress Wu to present an imperial offering to the High Heavens on top of the Tai Mountains.

Toward the end of *The Conspiracies of the Empire*, Judge Dee himself was also disgusted with the fact that, like others, he had to write the investigation report to Empress Wu in such an obsequious way, full of fulsome flatteries to the female dictator. Hence, the above-mentioned poem is excluded from this appendix – except for the one poem supposedly written by Judge Dee at the end of his investigation of the Luo Binwang case, though the authorship remains open to question.

The other inclusion is a poem written by Tang dynasty poet Chen Tao. Chen's lines influenced Judge Dee's decision as he maneuvered through this difficult investigation.

Call to Arms

Luo Binwang (626–687?)

This despicable woman surnamed Wu, an illegal usurper of the throne of the great Tang Empire, is evil incarnate. Born of a low-class family, she once served as a palace lady and took outrageous advantage of being close to Emperor Taizhong in private. After Taizhong's death, disregarding any ethical considerations, and concealing the favor the late emperor had showered on her, she shamelessly developed a scandalous relationship with Gaozong – the crown prince turned emperor – in secret.

Envious of all the other palace women, she became coquettish, bewitching, vindictive and wanton like a female fox. She soon secured the new emperor's exclusive favor in bed. Eventually, she seduced Gaozong into promoting her to the position of empress, with all its splendors, thereby precipitating him into an ugly incestuous situation.

She had a heart as venomous as a devilish snake, gathering vicious people around her, persecuting the royal and the noble, killing the brothers and sisters of the Li family, conspiring against the princes and poisoning the former Empress Wang.

Wu is consumed by her wicked ambition to become the supreme, unchallengeable ruler of the whole empire. She has imprisoned the crown prince in the palace and placed her own relatives, and the Wu family's running dogs, in the empire's most important positions.

Alas, a loyal premier, like Huo Guang of the Han Empire, will never appear again, and mighty royal family members, like Liu Zhang, have vanished out of sight. When the folk song 'Swallows Pecking at the Princes' was heard all over the country, people knew for sure that the Han Empire was coming to an end. When an evil dragon began drooling around the palace, it was an unmistakable harbinger of the demise of the Jin Empire.

I, Xue Jinye, a devoted and dutiful subject of the Tang Empire, have been long bathing in its graces, and as the eldest son of a noble family, I have long been observing the precious instructions left by the late emperor.

In ancient times, Song Weizi was not wrong to feel sad over the ruins of his country, and Huan Tan was not without his reasons to weep for losing his noble status. So now, full of indignation, I am determined to do something for the stability of the grand Tang Empire.

With the general disappointment about her rule prevailing under the sun, with warm support coming from all over our immense land, I raise high the flag of justice. And I pledge to sweep out the evils harming the great Tang Empire.

From faraway Baiyu in the south to the Three Rivers in the north, our numerous iron-clad steeds and chariots are stretching out all the way to the distant horizon. Corn is piling up high in storage in Hailing, and the grains are fermenting and turning red; the supplies in our warehouses are truly boundless. With flags streaming, over by the great river, how can the glorious achievement of restoring the grand Tang Empire still be far away? Stallions are neighing in the north wind, swords are shining up to the stars, and our soldiers' shouting is shaking the mountains and astonishing the skies. When we fight the enemies with all this, what enemies cannot be beaten by us? When we launch our brave attacks with all this, what cities cannot be taken by us?

Some of you are nobles who have enjoyed the glorious grace of the Tang Empire for generations; some are relatives of royal families, or are top-ranking officials who promised to execute the late emperor's will. With his words still sounding in our ears, how can you forget your mission of loyalty? Alas, while the soil on the late emperor's tomb is not yet dry, the young crown prince has already been exiled out of sight.

If you could turn the tables, however, and bid a proper farewell to the late emperor, remember his will, serve under his successor, the new emperor, with dedication, and gather together to preserve the great Tang Empire's Li royal family line, you will be granted knighthoods and rewards by the glorious throne that will run as long as the Yellow River, stand as solid as the Tai Mountains.

If you merely look at your feet, and hesitate at the crucial moment without seeing all the potent signs, severe punishment will surely fall to you.

See the picture clearly: today's world is being grasped in whose hand? This 'Call to Arms' will be distributed to all the provinces and counties, so all the people shall know.

This is one of the most inspiring, influential works of classical Chinese literature. Luo Binwang is known for the intertextual richness of his works. In this powerful 'Call to Arms', literary allusions are used abundantly. While this is a common feature among classical Chinese poets, it's so frequently employed in the 'Call to Arms' that readers may actually encounter a couple of allusions in every paragraph. In addition to that, parallel rhetoric is often used, too, which makes the brilliant piece even more impressive. The two overlap throughout the 'Call to Arms'.

In translating this mighty statement composed by Luo Binwang, I've met with several problems. For one, is it absolutely necessary to provide notes for each and every allusion for non-Chinese readers, at the expense of the reading flow? I opted not to take the academic approach, as long as the implied meaning of the allusions is understandable through context. And I have taken the same approach to the issue of parallel rhetoric.

Ode to a Goose

Luo Binwang (626–687?)

‘Goo, goo, goo!’
Arching its neck,
the goose is singing
to the high skies,
white feathers drifting
over the green water,
and red webs pedaling
in the clear ripples.

Ode to a Cicada in Prison

Luo Binwang (626–687?)

In the fall, you begin to sing
to a captive overwhelmed by worries.
It is unbearable to hear you scratching
your black wings in a sad song
to a white-haired prisoner like me.
The autumn dew drops falling,
falling too heavy, you cannot fly high.
The cold wind drowns your melody.
Who comes to believe you're so noble
and pure? Who comes to address
all the grievous wrongs afflicted
on an innocent man like me?

Remembering a Beautiful Girl in Shu

Luo Binwang (626–687?)

East and West, Wu and Shu, so far away
with passes and mountains standing
in the way. Alas, it is too far
for the letter-carrying fish to reach you,
or for the message-bearing wild goose.

Little wonder about the long streaks
of tears on your face, as you recall
the moment that the passionate clouds
turned into hot rain, circling,
caressing in the deep mountains.

To a Fishing Girl

Luo Binwang (626–687?)

A drunk traveler, lone, wet, cold,
boarded a sampan on a stormy night,
hungry like a wolf, where a young, pretty
fishing girl welcomed him, kneeling,
wearing a wet *dudou*-like corset
hugging the rise of her breasts,
her feet bare, silver bangles jingling,
lighting up the bamboo boat wall
behind her. She was making a vivid introduction
to the celebrated chef's special
of her sampan, waving the menu
in her hand, explaining the secret recipe
for frying a live mandarin fish.
A large one, with its head and tail sticking
out of the sizzling oil, was frying
in the wok, still turning, trembling.

A small smudge stuck on the arch
of her bare, shapely foot struck his imagination
and he experienced the hallucination
of her turning into a struggling fish
being scooped out of the net.
'Fry just for one minute,
better with an ice cube in its mouth.'

Served under the bamboo awning
of the boat, it tastes so tender, juicy,
melting on the tongue, its eyes goggling
once or twice – or was that something
he imagined in his intoxication?

The fish is turning back into the girl,
bleeding, struggling and thrashing, he
fell to suckling hard at her delicious, delicate toe
like a dainty ball of the fish-cheek meat.

The authorship of the poem is open to question.

In the Army

Luo Binwang (626–687?)

Beholden to the great favor from the Lord,
the whole army is full of courage.
The sunlight shining so bright
on the glaring double-edged lances
in the battlefield, the stars appearing
to engrave patterns on the swords.
Our full-stretched bows frame
the moon of the Han Empire,
our steeds stamp like thunder
on the barbarian land with swirling dust.
Caring not about what may happen to us
we are ready to lay down our lives
in return for our Lord's immense favor.

Seeing Off Officer Zheng at the Border

Luo Binwang (626–687?)

Facing the barbarian invasion from the enemy,
our heroic soldiers are marching east,
crossing Shanggan River to defend the country.
The shining arrows keep shooting, tearing
through the dense green willow leaves,
over the white-jade-decorated saddles,
against a blaze of blossoming peach flowers.
The bright moon projects the shadows
of the full-stretched bows to the ground,
with stars gathering around the tip
of the gigantic sword suspended in the sky.

Oh, don't be like a failed assassin
in the ancient times, singing,
in vain, the sad, sentimental song
of 'Chilly Wind by Yi River'.

Seeing Off a Friend by Yi River

Luo Binwang (626–687?)

Here, the brave assassin Jin Ke
bid farewell to his lord Prince Yan,
his hair bristling with indignation.
All the heroic and the gallant deeds
of the past long gone, the water
of the Yi River remains bone-chilling.

Jin Ke is a recurring figure in Luo's poems, and in classic Chinese poetry too. Jin made a brave assassination attempt on King Zheng of the Qin state, who was on the brink of conquering all parts of China and becoming the First Qing emperor. Jin sang a heroic song by the Yi River, where he parted with his friends before setting out on what he knew was an impossible, fatal mission.

Climbing the City Wall with the Army

Luo Binwang (626–687?)

The mighty troop on the city wall
sending a chill into the heart
of the enemy, the river water rising
with the cold-blooded message,
I'm going to the battle, wearing
the army uniform. In triumph,
I'll enter the capital of Chang'an
amidst the people singing and dancing.

Farewell to a Friend

Luo Binwang (626–687?)

The hour-knocking stretches the cold, long night,
The cool, clear sky spreads like in the cool autumn,
What present should I give you at our parting?
My heart, ice-pure in a clear jade vase.

Borders

Jiong Yang (650–695?)

How ferocious, furious the war rages on
north of Sai, how bitter, hard the battle
unfolds south of the city. The flags flapping,
stretching out like splendid wings,
the armor reflecting like silver scales
in the sun, the freezing water stinging
the steeds, and the sad autumn wind
worrying the people engaged in the war,
our generals and soldiers are infused
with the sunshine in their hearts, marching,
marching to the sand-covered borders
thousands and thousands of miles away.

Army Song

Jiong Yang (650–695?)

The beacon fire already reaching the Western Capital,
our hearts are full of indignation.
Bidding farewell to the palace,
the general leaves with the emperor's order,
and the soldiers fight bravely against the enemy
surrounding and attacking our city.
The heavy snow eclipsing the banners,
the battle drums adding to the howling wind.
O, I would rather be a petty officer fighting
than a useless scholar writing.

Lotus Flowers in the Winding Lake

Lu Zhaolin (634–686)

The light fragrance of the lotus flowers comes
circling the winding lake under the cover
of lush, round lotus leaves
upon lush, round lotus leaves. I am
worrying about the too-early arrival
of the autumn winds. Before you can
even fully appreciate the floral abundance
in the lake, thc flowers and leaves
may start falling, fading . . .

Double Nine Festival on the Mountains

Lu Zhaoling (634–686)

We climbed up the mountain to look out
on the day of the double nine festival . . .

A wave of homesickness is overwhelming
like the wind, and waves of dust rising
before our eyes. Alone, drinking
the golden chrysanthemum wine
in another land, I'm watching
a solitary wild goose flying
through the long, forlorn sky.

We cannot help feeling the same,
as if suspended under its wings.

The Double Nine Festival occurs on the ninth day of the ninth month in China's lunar calendar. In the Tang dynasty, people would observe the time-honored traditions of gathering together, climbing mountains and drinking chrysanthemum wine.

Missing Friends in the Cool Night

Wang Bo (650–676)

Morning after morning, I stand alone
under the verdant mountains, dusk
after dusk, I visit the blue river,
humming an unforgettable tune
from my old home. Oh, how I have
come to the familiar scenes, missing
the dear ones far, far away,
looking forward to the moment
of raising our cups together, sharing
the excitement over the fragrant greenness.

In the Mountains

Wang Bo (650–676)

The Yangtze River sings for me
in sorrow, as if with hiccups
amidst its endless flowing.
A lonely traveler thousands of
miles away cannot wait
for his return home. How much
more so in the evening,
with the wind bidding
farewell to the autumn,
with the yellow leaves swirling
all over hills and dales.

Seeing Off Du to His New Post in Shu

Wang Bo (650–676)

The three grand Qing cities
guarding the great capital of Chang'an,
in the background, here I am,
seeing you off, visualizing
you traveling all the way
through the wind and the mist
to your new post. The moment
of parting comes, so emotional,
at the beginning of our career
stretching out.
With a good friend,
located as far as the end
of the world, we still feel
close, like next-door neighbors.
Oh, don't break down, sentimentally
sobbing like young people,
at the sight of the road
forking in front of us.

Red Pomegranate Skirt

Wu Zetian (624–705)

Missing you in tears, day
and night, I was so devastated,
seeing scarlet as green in a trance—

'Incredible!' You take out my red
pomegranate skirt from the trunk
to double-check the tear stains.

Wu Zetian was summoned into the royal palace as a palace lady under the reign of the first Tang Emperor Taizhong. After his death, she was put into a Daoist nunnery, where she secretly carried on with the former crown prince – the new Emperor Gaozhong – and composed the above poem. In it, she suggests that she missed him so much while he was away that she mixed up the colors red and green, and challenges him to check her skirt for evidence of her tears. Their secret affair represented a huge 'incestuous' scandal to intellectuals like Luo Binwang at the time, who specifically denounced it in the 'Call to Arms', a declaration composed during the rebellion led by Xu Jingye against Empress Wu.

The Inscription on the Robe Given to Dee Renjie

Wu Zetian (624–705)

> An incorruptible mainstay
> of the great Tang Empire,
> you have stood so solid,
> working hard and diligently
> in your prominent position.
> The best example you are
> to all your colleagues.

For an official, it was considered an extraordinary honor to be given a robe by Empress Wu, particularly one with her inscription on it. Judge Dee was one such official, who was trusted by her. She was said to have broken down, weeping bitterly, on Judge Dee's death, declaring in heartbroken sadness, 'Look at the imperial court now. It is so empty, desolate!' Afterward, when confronted with difficult issues of the empire, she would exclaim, 'Why should the Old Heaven have deprived me of my most capable Premier Dee?'

Farewell to a Goose

Di Renjie (630–700)

Across the Han Dynasty bridge,
under the Tang Dynasty sun
we are going to part, like
the plum blossom unfolding out
in a white paper fan, like
the distant horizon sinking
on a black crow's wing,
as the weeds start swinging,
unexpectedly, to an unfamiliar tune.
Bubble of wrigglers
bursting on the green water.

The authorship of the poem is in question.

By the Wuding River

Chen Tao (812–885)

Pledged to wipe out the Huns,
they fought without any thoughts
for themselves, and died,
all of them, five thousand
sable-clad warriors, lost
in the dust of the North.

Alas, the white bones scattered there
by the faraway Wuding River,
still come in spring to haunt women's dreams,
in the shapes of their dead lovers.

Bamboo Twig Song

Liu Yuxie (772–842)

The willow shoots green,
the river water smooth,
she hears him singing
across the waves.

It shines in the east,
it rains in the west.

It is said not to be fine,
but it really is fine to me.

These poems were originally written and performed as folk songs in the early Tang period, when such poets as Luo Binwang, Wang Bo, Jiong Yang and Lu Zhaoling were active. Later on, a well-known mid-Tang-period poet, Liu Yuxie, edited and revised them. In The Conspiracies of the Empire, *Little Swallow is known for singing these songs in her sampan, and she was killed after singing them for Judge Dee.*

Bamboo Twig Song

Liu Yuxie (772–842)

Red peach blossoms blaze
all over the mountains
with the green spring waters
of the Shu River circling.

The flowers will easily fade,
my lord, like your passion,
while the water flows on,
never-ending, like my feelings.

Willow Shoots Song

Liu Yuxie (772–842)

The Qing River meanders
against myriads of willow shoots.
The scene remains unchanged
just like two decades ago . . .

This same old wooden bridge,
where I parted with her,
brings no news, alas,
no news for today.

The Song to the Stamp Dance

Liu Yuxie (772–842)

The bright moon gleaming
over the spring river,
the water rising to the big bank,
young girls were walking there
hand in hand.

Stamping, singing
through the new songs,
they failed to see their boyfriends there –
Only the green trees standing out
against the red morning clouds
with partridges warbling.